A

"Let's drink
head like a st
hand on whatever it was.

He took it, we shook hands again, and in shaking hands across a table I had never sat at, on an island I'd never been to, sitting with a man I'd never known, something set as strong as any mortar...."

A STORM AT SEA...

"On the bridge-wing it was like winter, one of those mornings with no wind and frost, and when I looked across the sea to port it was something to take your breath away. Out there, in a line along the horizon, was a wall..."

"...It was long and gray, black in places like the bands people wear around their arms, like some kind of curtain rising from the bottom of the sky, and it had come from nowhere...."

A DANGEROUS RESCUE...

Something terrible was going to happen, maybe to him, certainly to somebody....

"Are you sure you want to go on with this?" I said.

He got up and walked back to where he had been before, six feet or so from the sea....

"Of course," he said. "You have to go to the end, don't you?"

RESCUE

a novel based on a true story

by
George V. Packard

G&G Publications
USA

Paperback edition published by
G&G Publications
PO Box 18, Whately, MA 01093 USA
Bulk orders available.

ISBN-13: 978-1456419486
ISBN-10: 145641948X

Cover Art: "Breaking Wave" by Kordula Packard,
used with permission.
Cover & Book Design by Gail Cleare

For Kordula and for my children
Stephen, Cynthia, Leslie,
Susan and Michael.

RESCUE

PROLOGUE

West from Bimini the Gulf Stream moves north faster than a man walks. Half a mile deep and fifty miles wide, on its surface yellow weed drifts, headed for the Sargasso Sea. A ship crossing to the west trails a white wake, dark blue around the wake, around the ship, a deep indigo off Bimini and alone and ahead there is a line in the sea.

From the bridge of the ship the line lays across the bow and past it is another blue, pale and cornflower. And as the line passes beneath something should happen, a sound, an alarm, but nothing happens and the ship crosses the edge of the Stream.

To starboard the sea buoy rocks in the swell, clanging red chimes, a rusted, triangular king. The cans and nuns nod black and red and the stone jetties flank the way home.

Behind the ship the line in the sea divides the two blues, pale cornflower and indigo, the end of a continent and the edge of the Stream, moving north faster than a man walks.

PART ONE

I

There is no darker night than a cloud covered one below latitude thirty-degrees north. It's a blanket pulled over your head, with no wind a sack with the cord drawn tight, and it was that kind of night I met him. Literally ran into him trying to find my way back to the harbor, to the boat and my bunk. One foot in front of the other like a drunk I walked down the black-topped road, feeling with my feet for the potholes, my hands out in front of me like a blind-folded man, and there he was, standing in the middle of the road.

He was there all right, you could be sure of that. A man you wouldn't forget, too, six feet four or five of him and solid as a rock in the dark. And the first time I met him, the first time and the last, I didn't even see him.

I felt him, his arm, a shoulder, with my hands like a blind man.

"Excuse me," I said, and started around to the right, changed my mind and went left and ran into him again. He hadn't moved. He was still standing there in the dark in the middle of a road.

"I couldn't see you," I said and was sure I should go, and soon, get around him one way or another, because why should a man be standing in the road, a road full of holes, when you couldn't see your hand in front of your face?

But I didn't go.

I stood there in the black and waited for him to speak, and then I said,

"Are you all right?"

I was sure he wasn't, knew it even without seeing him, but I wasn't sure he heard me. I could have been talking to the right or left of him, only speaking to the night.

"Can I help you?" I said, and then he spoke.

"No...it isn't anything...," was what he said.

But it wasn't true. There was something, someone else perhaps, behind him, more than just us two. You could feel it all around us.

Whatever it was, it was there, as if we had both brought something, or someone, to a meeting in the road. But just then, standing in the dark, there were only the two of us.

"Are you staying here, on the island?" I said, but he didn't answer.

"Are you at the hotel?"

"Yes," he said, "I'm staying there," but he

said it as if he didn't want to stay, or say it, either.

"I'm going that way," and I spoke as if I was. "I'll walk with you if we can find the way."

"I can find the way," he said, and he started up the road.

I followed him, back the road I had come, and right away I stumbled, but he did know the way, as if he had walked there more than once in the dark. And we found the hotel, saw the yellow lanterns in the garden, smelled the heavy flowers blooming in the dark.

We went into the bar, into the light that was there, the candles on the tables, lighted glasses behind the bar. The calypso singer was gone and his drums in a corner. The varnished wood of the walls and the floor shone in the shadows and the only thing to see was the lines of lighted glasses and the bartender's jacket, white and buttoned to the neck. Below his cuffs and above the collar he was as brown as the wood on the walls and he nodded when we came in. He nodded to the man I followed.

I thought coffee and cognac would give him a choice and said we should sit down, but he didn't hear me. I took his arm and pointed to a table. In the light of the candles, the shining from behind the bar, you could see him now, with a face you would remember.

We sat, finally, at some table he chose and I looked at the couple in the corner. They were not to be seen unless you were looking, sitting side by side and hand in hand. People came to Bimini for that I knew and others came for the fishing, but they were young and not looking at us.

And the man across the table from me, I couldn't even guess.

He had walked up the King's Highway in the dark, a real dark, as if he had walked it more than once, not missing a turn, as if he had walked it when there had been a King.

"Are you sure you're all right?" I said. "That's a dangerous road in the dark. You could fall in a hole."

He nodded, and then he smiled, not the best kind of smile but the kind you gave. It didn't surprise me. I had seen it before, waiting in a barbershop or standing at a bar. And we didn't look the smallest bit alike, him with a face that might have been carved somewhere, blue eyes, curly gray hair all over his head; and me, narrow with ears, hair straight back, neat as a pen in a holder.

"You've been here before?" I said.

"Yes, I've been here often,' he said.

"For the fishing?"

"No."

"Just to get away from it all."

"No, you couldn't say that," he said and for a moment it looked as if he would really smile, but he didn't and then he said,

"No, that is something you really couldn't say."

I was going to suggest he came to stand in the road. I thought he might laugh if I did.

"Not just to stand in the road, either," he said and I laughed at a coincidence I was sure was not. You either believe in them or you don't and I hadn't in a very long time. Not believing in coincidences is a matter of infinite hope and you either believe in that or you don't.

"My name is Richardson," I said and offered my hand across the table, ...Robert." I smiled and we shook hands.

"Farrington," he said, "Francis O...."

"This is my first time here," I said. "Some people I know have a boat."

"You're interested in that?"

"No, I don't get on very well with boats," I said quickly. "But I've never been here before."

He sat back in his chair and drank from his drink. Then he set it on the table.

"I come every year," he said and I wanted to say 'why?' but I didn't. Most people would have but I didn't. I knew it was the right thing not to say.

How I knew that then, so early, I don't know but I did. Later there was another chance to say the wrong thing and that chance I took.

We sat and said nothing, sipped the cognac and let the coffee go cold.

In the silence it was as if I had said, 'why?' to his, 'I come every year.' As if he had heard me think it.

"And you never fish?" I said. It was laughable but what else could I ask him?

"No, people come here for that and for...."

And I did say, "What?"

It was the first time but it wasn't the last.

Later it seemed to be the only word I could say and not be wrong.

"They come for better reasons," he said and I looked at the couple in the corner. They were the same, not looking at us.

"I can see why they do. It's antique in a way."

"What is?"

"The island, as if it had seen better days and liked them better, too."

"I've heard that before, something like it...anyway," he said and put his hands on the arms of the chair. He looked around the room, looked around to see where he had heard it, but it wasn't there.

"I'm not very original," I said.

"No, I didn't mean that," he said. "I only meant..." and that was all he said.

We watched the couple. They were watching each other and we were looking at them. I hoped what I always hoped, that they were two of a kind, enough to open with anyway.

"Would you like another drink?" I said.

"Yes," and he nodded.

The bartender saw, not looking he saw.

"Are you sure you're all right?" I said. "There might be a doctor somewhere."

"There's nothing wrong," he said, "...nothing." He was looking at his hands, first one and then the other, as if they had something to do but had forgotten what it was. Then he picked up his glass and finished it. "There are only witch-doctors here, anyway," he said and smiled, a little, enough, just enough so you knew he remembered how.

"How are they?"

"The witch-doctors?"

"Yes."

"Average," he said and we laughed.

It was the first time and I held up my glass, "At the other end of the island they come to drink, or so I'm told," I said. "You know that place, 'The End Of The World Bar,' some name like that?" and I finished my glass.

He drank from his glass but it was just like the fishing. He didn't fish, didn't look like he drank, and as for the couple in the corner you couldn't be sure, not absolutely, but sure enough there was no one waiting.

"Let's drink on it," I said, the drink climbing in my head like a sunrise.

"On what?"

"On whatever," I said, "on whatever it means," and standing up I offered my hand on whatever it was.

He took it, we shook hands again, and in shaking hands across a table I had never sat at, on an island I'd never been to, sitting with a man I'd never known, something set as strong as any mortar.

I thought it had. That it hadn't couldn't have entered my mind. And it didn't until a long time after when I knew it was hardly me he was talking to at all.

I thought there was a tattered banner in the wind, or a crooked trumpet sounded, that it was finally time, that he had heard. And not because he was standing in the road, because I had asked if he was ill or needed help, none of those.

It was because I hadn't been afraid.

That he could not have known it, could not have known I was not afraid, was inconceivable, for as well as I he must have known there is nothing to be afraid of when there is nothing left to fear.

"Farrington and Richardson," I said, "it could be…."

"It could be what?" he said.

"Hung on a door?"

"Hung in any case," he said and there was that slice of a smile upon which I was to wager so much.

I laughed, more than I should have, more than what he had said deserved, but my head was full of sunrises and because for me, right then and there, we were surely two of a kind at that table. Jacks at least, I thought, enough to open in any man's game.

We were a matched pair in a gaitless world, a world where I had thought up to then that if you knew anything at all it was — know thyself and trust nobody, and fear all.

But I suppose he might have known, for a moment anyway. He knew enough about it to know. But not by looking at what was sitting across from him because there was nothing much to see. Small and unattached, glasses and the beginnings of a paunch. Just the same he might have, he knew about it and he looked like it, too, hunched like a bear in that chair, his hand around his glass so you couldn't see the glass, staring across a room at nothing I could see but he could see too well.

He might have and sometimes, still, I like to think he did.

We had another drink and another after that, and I said,

"You come here every year."

And he said,

"Yes."

And after walking in the dark, much later at the end of an island, he said it again — "I come here every year." —knowing I would say, "Why?"

II

He would answer, too, not there and not then, and not in a few words either, but he would, all in the darkest kind of night, but not the darkest we had seen.

He answered after I told him about me, as if that was how it had to be. It was some kind of contract that came after the handshake, I thought, and I told him, not everything, but nearly everything, all that water over the dam but none of it off a duck's back — all you could tell another person.

And much later when I knew what had happened, when I knew everything that meant anything to him, I wished I had told him all there was to tell.

A long time afterwards, and even now, I wish I had. It might have made a difference.

Not to him, of course, but to me. It might have made a difference to me.

But I don't tell much of a story, even when I have to, even when it's not the truth. People fall off like soldiers on the march, one at a time, and sit by the road, and if the story is long enough, at the end I'm marching along all by myself.

And he listened to it, every word, I'm sure he did sitting in that chair hunched over in some kind of brown jacket with a pipe in his pocket he couldn't smoke or wouldn't work.

I told him the lot, nearly, and lastly how now that I could, reasonably, start thinking of the end I had pulled in my lines, drawn them into an interior form like a limpet on a rock. And by then inebriate of metaphor, how I was flanked by Maginots, my Munichs so long ago they were far enough away to be forgotten.

He didn't argue. People would have, most

people would, but not as advocates for me. They would have their own defenses: 'But there were the good times,' and there were. 'We always remember the bad,' and we do, but there is more to it than good and bad. One of the things man does best is to divide by two. What you remember is how it was, and he didn't say, 'What about the good times?' He didn't say anything at all but marched with me right to the end.

"And that's what the bear found on the other side of the mountain," I said, and wondered what he had found on the other side of his.

"And the man in the road?" he said.

"Another man in the dark," and this time he really did laugh, but it was not at what I said. He laughed at my presumption, at what I thought was 'dark,' when he knew a kind I would never know.

But if you want to, and I did, you hear what you listen for, even in laughter, and I still heard the crooked trumpet and saw the battered banner. We rode stirrup to stirrup, I thought, with all that one man could tell another between us, but in that, of course, I was wrong.

In the long night he told me much more. He told me because I was standing there beside him, but only because I was there. Perhaps just anyone would not have served; I often think of that, but it wasn't me he told.

By the time I was finished we had done in the bottle. The couple in the corner was gone and the bartender was putting out the candles one after the other all around the empty room. He didn't make any noise and neither did the candles, I thought. In his white jacket buttoned to the neck the service was over and I hadn't even noticed when the couple left.

"I didn't see them go," I said.

He was standing up now. It seemed as if

he was standing on the chair but his feet were on the floor. I looked to see if they were there and they were.

"Didn't see who?" he said.

"The people, when they left."

"They didn't see you, either," he said and there was something else in his voice, something that had not been there before, not sharp but not dull either.

"Gone fishin', you think?"

"No, I don't think so," he said and finished his glass standing up.

Outside, there was the beginning of a moon and breaks in the clouds, tears in the sky where the winds blew high up, and we stood in the sand looking at the pewter sea. It was cooler, too, with a breeze down on the water. We stood there and looked out as far as you could see, along a line of silver, west toward the rest of the world.

I felt fine, better than I had felt for as long as I could remember, emptied out like the bottle we had finished. I had told my story and he had 'stayed the route' was what we used to say, and as we walked along the beach I sang, the cognac sang and I kept time with my feet,

"I HAD A GOOD HOME AND I LEFT, YOU'RE RIGHT.

I HAD A GOOD HOME AND I LEFT, YOU'RE RIGHT."

It was all I could remember of it and maybe there wasn't even any more of it to remember and I was going to sing it again but he said,

"Were you in the service?'

"I was."

"Army?"

"The United States Army," I said. "I did my duty," and then I remembered the rest of, 'I Had A Good Home And I Left,'

"SOUND OFF: ONE, TWO, THREE, FOUR

ONE -- TWO – THREEFOUR!

I thought to myself I could do this all night, just march along the beach singing, "ONE -- TWO -- THREE – FOUR," and then I heard him say beside me,

"What did you think of it?"

"What?"

"Duty," he said.

"What did I think of it?" I said because I didn't know what I thought of it and because I felt so fine, my head cleaned out and clear, master of all he surveyed, I said,

"If necessity is the staff life beats you with, duty is what you do," and I wanted to shake hands with myself. I tried it. I tried to shake hands with myself but it didn't work. And all he said to that was,

"Anything happen?"

"Where?"

"In the army. You didn't say you had done anything like that."

"That was the part that was excluded because I forgot it," I said, "the part of the middle that wasn't there."

"And anyway," I said, "nothing happens in the army, except you learn how to eat out of a can with your fingers. I typed. I was a demon at it, Demon Clerk Typist Second Class. Forms, more forms than you ever saw in your life and what do you mean, did anything happen?"

He didn't want to hear about it. He was watching the sea as we walked. The line of the moon kept step with us, a line you could walk down if you knew how and the cognac and I wondered if the moon had a good home and it left.

We walked and then he stopped. It was no special place but he stopped and the only thing you could hear was the sea touching the shore.

He turned to me,

"Do you know there's a river out there," he said

"Out where?"

"There" he said, and he waved his hand south from the Windward Islands — north to Cape Hatteras and Labrador.

I didn't know what to say. I thought again that there might be something wrong with him because there may have been a river out there if you went far enough, but we were standing on a beach, on the edge of an ocean. I had to say something so I said,

"There's water enough."

"There's water enough all right," he said, "more than a man can imagine, and moving, too."

"The Gulf Stream," I said.

"Yes, and moving faster than a man walks, if he could. He can't so he swims, and if he can't do that — he drifts."

"In the stream in the ocean?"

"Yes," he said and began to walk again.

I thought about someone drifting in an ocean, and then just about drifting and it sobered me, those drifters in waterways and rivers and streams. We were in one now, the two of us, an eddy on the edge of one anyway, and tomorrow we would be off again down a river they say is never the same but is always the same. I felt my old chill come back from where it had been, walking along behind me.

"Here," he said, and stopped.

"What?"

"Near enough to here, anyway."

He was digging the sand with his foot, the end of his shoe. I thought there might be something buried there and started to go down on my hands and knees to dig with my hands.

"Here?" I said and pointed down at the sand.

"No, out there for God's sake," he said and waved his hand again across the water.

He was standing with his legs apart.

"The thing looks just the same," he said.

"There's nothing different about it, ever."

"What looks the same?" I said.

"That," and this time he didn't wave, he pointed.

He pointed at an ocean, arm straight out from the shoulder as if he wanted it to leave the room, the house, the earth.

"I've been looking at it for a long time," he said and let his arm drop. It fell against his side, the hand open.

"Too long a time," he said. "I don't count, but this was where we came."

And I couldn't believe it. So that was what it was going to be, 'This was where we came.' I would never have guessed it. I was sure it was going to be more than that, much more. It had never entered my mind it could be a woman.

And in the end I was right. I wasn't right about much that night but I was about that. There was a woman in it all right, but that's all she was — in it. She wasn't what was behind him, out there from the Windward Islands to Labrador, even if he thought so.

He was facing me now, trying to see my face, as if it were important to see it when he said,

"You see I thought I was right."

He came closer to me,

"I thought it was right because it was the truth. People do tell the truth, you know, some people do."

"They do?" I said, remembering that I had tried to and couldn't, not all the truth, not all there was. And anyway, truth and lies were something I thought I knew something about. I had learned in the hardest of ways that no one should fear the lie that is told; what you should fear is the truth not said.

And I said it again,

"They do?" but he didn't hear me or he didn't want to and we were walking again. He was looking straight out in front of him as if he was going someplace now.

I walked faster to be beside him.

"What was it?" I said.

He didn't answer and I asked again,

"What did you tell her?"

"The truth about it," he said. "Exactly the truth about it, …about something that happened."

"When?"

"When?" he said.

"Yes."

"While you were typing and eating out of a can. While you were doing that, things were happening, you know. Important things. Things that changed everything."

"In the service?" I said and he laughed. It had the same sound about it as when I had told him about the army and said something about, '…duty.' He was laughing at the words.

"Yes, in the service," he said and waved his hand at the sea again, waving it to him or waving it away, I couldn't tell.

"Before I met her, when we were serving, remember? ...We were on a search...we were out much further than I thought."

I didn't say anything. Now I would just wait because there was more, much more from out there where the ocean rolled from one end of the world to the other.

And then there were rocks on the beach in front of us, a pile of them where somebody had tried to build something to keep the sea away. Whoever it was had never finished or it hadn't worked because there was just a long pile of them there from the water to the trees. They weren't doing anything, keeping the sea in or out, they were only in the way and if we wanted to keep going we would have to climb.

"Shall we go on?" I said.

"What did you say?"

"I said shall we go on?"

"That's something we do, isn't it?" and he

started up over the rocks.

"Yes, that's something we do," and I began to climb behind him.

I could have said that I was tired, that it didn't make sense to stay up all night and walk around on a beach. It was a chance and perhaps I should have taken it because then, walking back to the hotel I could have said, "Half the world are women, you know, more than half," and that would have been all there was to it. But we kept going, and before he was finished there was nothing for me to say at all.

We climbed the rocks and went on, like boys with a stick and a ball. I'd had my turn and now it was his. It didn't matter if it was late and you could hardly see the ball.

III

"You were in love with her?" I said.

"In love with her?"

"Yes."

"Everyone says those words."

"They say everyone does."

"They don't mean the same to everyone," he said. "They don't mean the same to me."

And what can you say to that?

I said I understood, a little lie between friends, but really I understood it all right. The truth was I didn't believe it, but it wasn't going to make any difference if I believed it or not because he did, or at least he thought he did.

"And it was because of what happened . . .," and I started to wave my hand the way he had waved his, but I stopped.

"Yes," he said, "all because of what happened...when we were out there."

I looked at the sea, where some small waves ran with the wind. It had been there all along, next to us, marching along beside us and never saying a word.

"Not sixty miles from here," he said. "You could nearly see where if it was light."

"You remember just a place on the water?"

"I remember it all right. Twenty-seven north; seventy-nine, thirty-eight west."

It was somewhere two imaginary lines crossed on an ocean, on a map or a globe. It was only some numbers, not even a street address or a telephone number. It was a place on an empty ocean.

"Exactly that place?" I said.

"Yes, exactly there," he said and he began to walk faster again. I had to run to catch up.

"You were in the Navy?"

"Yes, the other Navy. Search and Rescue,

US Coast Guard, on the cutter that pa-
trolled here."

"But not in Bimini," I said.

"No, the ship moored in Port Everglades,
in Florida, but this was where we were, a
couple of hundred miles in every direction
from here anyway. One hour stand-by,
towing somebody in, pumping somebody
out, looking all over hell for somebody who
wasn't even there, some yachtsman sitting
in a bar somewhere.

He made a sound, it could have been his
laugh, and I turned to look at him.

"We never saved anybody, not really, except once. We saved him all right, maybe
we even saved two. We saved somebody,
anyway."

He was staring along the line of the island
in front of us, and then off toward the water. What moon there was came out of the
clouds, went back, came out again. In the
silver light the edge of his face, his hand, he

was holding it up in front of his face as if in a moment he would reach out, were cut into the dark like an etching.

"Not very far from here," he said, "but far enough to find out all you ever need to know," and he started to nearly run up the beach, one long stride after another as if he was going to run until there wasn't any more land left between him and that place on the water.

I followed him, and I did run to keep up. We left the shuttered beach houses behind, only black pine trees on our right, a narrow white passage of sand in front of us, and off to the left was the sea, still there beside us.

We came to the end of the island, if an island has an end. It's not very far and he stopped. I nearly reached out to grab him before he stopped. I was going to hold him if I could like some animal on a cliff, but I didn't have to. We slowed, and when his feet were almost in the water, he stopped and pointed.

"Right there," he said, "not sixty miles from here."

He began to tell me then. What had gone before was overture, and not even that because the girl, the woman, whatever she was, stood at the end. And not even at the end. She stood along the side a long way ahead like someone on the edge of a road.

"I was only out here because of the war," he said, "you remember that war. The one when they stood on a line of latitude and shot at each other and died doing that? Well, I didn't want to shoot or get shot at or die. I was in law school. I was trying to learn what law was, you understand that? It was going to be pretty damned stupid to be maimed or killed, dead forever shooting across a line you couldn't even see for reasons you couldn't understand.

"I enlisted, Officer's Candidate School, United States Coast Guard, a hundred and twenty day wonder they called us. They wanted you if you'd gone to college. They thought if you could pass a test you could do the things they wanted you to do, officer material they called it. Bring it in, put it together, stuff it with Celestial Navigation, Seamanship, Damage Control, Search and Rescue, fit it out with two little gold bars, and then push you out to see if you would float."

"We didn't belong out there anymore than you would because there were things that could happen that didn't have anything to do with seamanship or navigation. Somebody thought if you could go to college you could go to sea, and not on your hands and knees with a chipping hammer and a paint brush. They thought you could go standing straight up wearing a hat with a gold ribbon that meant you were in charge of people and always blew off in the wind.

"It was all in the books, they said, metacentric heights, azimuths, sidereal angles, the theoretical size of a catenary, breaking strength of line and cable and chain, we learned all that. The only thing we didn't know, they didn't know either — whether we could do it or not."

He stopped, maybe to catch his breath. What he had just said had come out as fast as it had because it had been waiting. For how long I never knew. I could have figured it out, though, the way women count months on their fingers.

I thought of what it must mean to be, '...in charge of people,' to be in some real way responsible for them. I had never been in charge of anybody except myself and what kind of a job had I done? And as far as being responsible for somebody? It was better not to think about that.

He turned to me standing beside him in the dark.

"Did you go to college?"

"Yes."

"What did you study?"

"Economics."

He made that sound again, a little like a laugh.

"They would have taken you, too. It could have been you out there just as well as me."

It was true. You go through different doors most of time, but that one could have been the same. It might have been him standing there, listening for whatever was going to happen.

"I came aboard the ship right out of Officer's Candidate School. Ensign Francis O. Farrington, service number 40884, with new uniforms, half-a-dozen cap covers, shined shoes and a salute like a British Grenadier. I walked up that gangway as the new Deck Officer; one day out and I was in charge of everything on the ship except the bridge and the engines. Only I wasn't."

"A piece of paper said I was and I had the title, 'First Lieutenant', but that was all I had. The Chief Bosun Mate had everything else."

"We had some of those officers, too," I said, "the same hundred and twenty day wonders. They were second-lieutenants and stood around most of the time."

"I stood around, too, just trying to keep out of the way, watching them chip and paint, coil and flemish line, lower the pulling boat and bring it back onboard. I knew what they were doing, we had learned that, but I couldn't have done it myself."

"Some of them were all right," I said. "We had a good one."

"Good at what?"

"Paper, a second lieutenant from an ROTC somewhere. He was good at paper."

"Christ, I could do paper," he said. "Do you know how much paper it takes to run a ship? Reports, files, requisitions, bills of lading, commissary, letters back and forth. I could do those and I did, yards of them, fathoms, and I didn't make any mistakes, either. If I was going to make one the Yeoman would say, 'Yes sir, Mr. Farrington, but ….' and that was enough. I knew enough to know that."

For a moment I was back in that time, too, with the sound of paper coming in and going out, roll it in, roll it out, tap, tap, tap. The smell of beer and khaki, a calendar on the wall that if you could only get to the end of you had it made. Back in a thing if you've never been in you would never believe.

There were people behind desks behind doors who knew your past, ordered your present, and wanted to plan your future, and though not in the same service as he, it had been the same time. It was just as he said, except for combat. That was not the same at all, they said, and I believed them.

"You didn't fight?" I said.

"No. I didn't and there was Coast Guard in the middle of it, landing craft, aids to navigation, river patrol and some of them got killed, but not us. We were trying to save people. Can you believe that? The law said you kill them or you save them. You did one or the other or you went to jail. They said it was an obligation."

"Insane," I said.

"It was, and I'll tell you something else — there were things that went on saving them just as crazy as killing them."

I believed it. A time comes when if you've seen enough you can believe anything, when the world really is a new ball game where the pitcher pitches straight up in the air and the batter beats the ground with his bat.

"I believe it," I said.

"You can, every mad part of it, because not too long after I came aboard our Executive Officer was transferred and the next day I was *him*, second in command of the Coast Guard Cutter Travis, one hundred and twenty-five feet of men and guns and machinery and search and rescue gear."

"They made me Executive Officer because I could send a letter out of that ship's office that was something, all the jargon in the right place, half a dozen references even if it was about a lost ball bearing, and a distribution list so everybody down at Commander Seventh Coast Guard District in Miami knew there was a hot-shot Exec aboard the CGC Travis."

" Records, personnel, monthly, bi-annual, annual reports and I knew where everything was on that ship, too, how much we had and how much we needed. I could do all that because you could add it and subtract it and make it come out."

"Right," I said, keeping my end up.

"You think so?"

"The only way," I said, "keep the confusion out."

He spoke before I had finished, and louder,

"Confusion! You don't know what that is."

"I don't?"

"No," and then softer, "but you couldn't know what I mean and neither did I. It wasn't in the books and I didn't learn it down in that ship's office, but I learned it."

I wondered what he meant. Everything of mine was in shoeboxes, plenty of them to begin with but fewer all the time. Now I had half-a-dozen and soon I knew I would be down to three, then two, and finally it would all fit in one box.

"What do you mean?" I said.

He had his hands in the pockets of his coat and with the moon behind the clouds he was just a shadow beside me.

"There's something else," he said, "something that doesn't fit, and when you find it you don't know where it goes."

I was going to ask him right then and there what it was, but I didn't. It was just like when he had said that he came here every year. It was the right thing to do not to ask.

"The only thing that really worried me I tried not to think about. It was the longest kind of chance anyway, the chance that we would have a rescue call in the middle of the night and the Captain couldn't make it. More than half the crew lived ashore and waited for the telephone to ring. They sat around in a living room somewhere and waited for the duty quartermaster aboard the ship to call and say: 'Priority message – Immediate departure' and hang up."

"Then the quartermaster would call the next one from his telephone log and only the Lord could help you if you were not at the other end of that number. If you left home to go anywhere, out to eat, to a bar, a movie, anywhere, you called the ship and left the number. And you could be called in some pretty strange places I can tell you. But I was afraid the Captain would have an accident on his way to the ship or his car wouldn't start or his phone wouldn't work because we didn't wait."

"We didn't wait for anyone, not even him. We had one hour to get away from that dock. A message went out the minute the last mooring line came aboard and they had both times down in Miami at Search and Rescue Operations, the time they called us and the time we called them and they could count to sixty."

"And I was second in command. If the Captain didn't make it I would have to take the ship out and go wherever we had to go, but he always made it. He never missed a ship in his life and there was a CO who did, a lieutenant on a ninety-three footer in

Miami, and they sent him to a rock somewhere on isolated duty. But not the Captain. He was always there, knew we were going to get a call even before we got it. It seemed as if he was there even when he wasn't."

At that he stopped, but only for a moment, took his hands out of his pockets and put them back again. When he did his pipe fell out, the one he couldn't smoke or didn't work. I picked it up and shook the sand off.

"Do you know anything about Captains?" he said.

"Nothing. I didn't know anything about Captains even in the Army, except you saw one from a distance once in a while."

"They're not the same thing. When someone becomes the Captain of a ship they become a different sort of person."

"What sort?" I said because as far as I was concerned a Captain was a Captain, someone who told other people to tell you what to do.

"A different sort altogether," he said. "I swear he knew we were going to get a call before we got it. I'd come running up that gangway at three or four o'clock in the morning and the quartermaster would throw me a salute and say, 'Captain's aboard, sir,' and he would be. He'd be up on the bridge shuffling charts around smoking his pipe with a cup of coffee and watching the clock and then he would say, 'Single-up all lines.' I don't know how he did it but he did and I had nothing to be afraid of."

He gave his laugh again, more of a bark than a laugh, and said,

"Nothing to be afraid of…nothing I knew anything about, anyway. No one had written it down on a piece of paper…so you could find it when you needed it."

"No," he said so softly I could hardly hear him, "I couldn't find it when I needed to. It didn't come with the Rules of the Road. It didn't come with anything. It just came...out of nowhere."

And then that laugh again, but this time it wasn't any sort of laugh I wanted to hear another time. It came out as much of a cry as a laugh with something crooked in it like hearing a rooster bark or a cat croak, and I looked around me. We were a long way from anywhere and there were only the dark trees behind us and the sea at our feet.

But I didn't believe things came out of nowhere. Everything comes from some-where, one way or another. I always told people that I wasn't born yesterday, or even again, but I stood there on the beach and listened to him because he believed it and part of our agreement, the one we had made by making none at all, was that there would be no argument.

He stopped talking and looked up into the sky. Most of the clouds were gone, blown to the edge of the earth, and the moon was out. Half of it was up there in the dark, and the other half, too, the half you couldn't see but knew was there. I stood beside him and looked up, trying to see the other half of the moon.

I offered him a cigarette, lit them both and we smoked, two red points of light under a thousand million white ones above us, and finally he spoke again,

"Do you believe in omens?"

"I don't think I do," I said.

"There was one."

"When?"

"Before it happened. I'm positive that was what it was."

"How do you know?"

He smoked with the red end of the cigarette in the cup of his hand.

"It was an omen all right," he said. "There were crew on that ship who had been stationed down here for years and never seen one."

"Seen what?" I said but he was seeing something he had seen once and in which I did not believe.

"And it was just like the other one, the one that came a day after it and I know you don't believe me but I swear to you it came from…nowhere."

The word hung in the air under that half of a moon like two beats of a drum, like two croaks of a raven, and then was gone.

IV

"We were half-way across the Gulf Stream from Lauderdale to Bimini escorting small boats, twenty-four of them, and it was slow. There wasn't much of a sea but enough to keep their speed down and they were like dogs on a leash. They wanted to get there, through that fifteen-foot wide entrance into the harbor, moor in that gin water, and start doing whatever it was they came to do, women, drinking, business, whatever forty or fifty men would do on a weekend in the Bahamas."

"They were on a conference or a meeting or escaping from wives, who knows, and we were there to see they got there and back. What they did ashore was their own business. We had to anchor outside anyway, we drew too much water for the harbor. We couldn't have gotten in there if we had to."

"You could see Bimini from the bridge-wing. The small boats couldn't see it yet, they were too low in the water, but we could, the white beach, this one right here, houses with orange roofs, the same trees. And down to the southeast past the Grand Bahama Bank there was a cloud in the sky, gray, the only one anywhere. It was just down there on the horizon left over from yesterday or too early for today. You could see all of it, the top and the edges the way you can see a fog bank off Maine or Nova Scotia, and then it wasn't sitting anymore."

"It was moving north-west, one cloud moving all by itself."

"The small boats saw it, too, and pushed up their throttles, straight east through that bright blue water with nothing but white cotton balls above them and coming from the right that bunch of gray like a hill of dirty sheets."

"We were a mile or two behind and I went over to the radar and put my head inside the hood. The boats were there on the screen, I could see all of them, count them, and there was Bimini out in front right where it should be. The radar was on the five-mile range and I set it on ten and there were the boats again, smaller and bunched together, with all of the island showing, and something else."

"It was a solid echo off to the right and nothing like sea return or a rain squall, bright white in the green of the screen and out in the ocean where there should have been nothing at all. And it was coming from right to left faster than anything else on the scope with just enough lead to meet us if we didn't change our course or speed."

"I felt the ship turn, to port, and everything on the screen turned too, a half-turn to the right. The Captain had changed course to the north and now the small boats were off to the right of us still moving in a bunch for the island, and the cloud, whatever it was, the blot at the bottom was off the sweep with a smudge of white coming into the green. Then the ship turned again and the island was behind us with more of that white smear off to the left and coming fast."

"It looked like the Captain didn't want anything to do with it because now we were around 180 degrees going back the way we had come. And I suppose you won't believe any of this, I wouldn't believe it myself, but that thing on the screen had changed direction too. It was still coming for us. It was out in front the way it had been when we were heading east. The damned thing had changed course, too, and it was getting closer."

"What was it?" I said. I couldn't be quiet any longer, but he didn't hear me. He was looking out across the black water and watching something move across the ocean.

"I'm telling you," he said, "you would swear to God it was following us. The Captain changed course twice after that, ninety-degree course changes, and that blot moved too. When we had settled down going north or east again it was there, off our bow or quarter and moving to meet us."

"You were sure it could think and I couldn't make up my mind to take my head out of the radar hood. It was dark in there, darker than it is right here, and in there you could imagine it wasn't happening. The might be something wrong with the equipment, a capacitor or a condenser that somebody could fix, but there was nothing wrong with the radar. When I took my head out and looked, it was real enough, as real as anything like that could be."

"What was out there?" I said.

"You hear about them," he said, "and there are stories. A meteorological anomaly they call it, but I had never seen one and neither had anyone else."

"What?" I said again because he wouldn't name it. If he didn't name it, would there be nothing there?

"An insane looking thing in the sky. A crooked, crazy ice cream cone staggering around on its end."

"An ice cream cone?"

"A waterspout, a tornado at sea. It went from the ocean up into the sky, up into that gray cloud like some kind of root and you could see it spinning, turning faster than anything you ever saw spin, and it was solid. I tell you it was as solid, as hard as the muscle of a man's arm."

"And there was a blur at the bottom, white water where the funnel touched, and the sea was torn up but everywhere else around us the sea was calm. There wasn't a wave over two feet anywhere you looked except at the base of that funnel. I tell you it was terrifying and disgusting at the same time, that thing up in the sky, gray and filthy. It didn't belong there, or anywhere else, and it changed direction when we did and followed us."

"Followed the ship?" I said hardly believing what I was saying.

"We'd turn and it would," he said, "leaned and staggered like a drunk and tall as a quarter of the sky. It leaned toward us or away but always with that funnel coming across the water tearing a hole in it and sucking up that gray tube."

"You can spend a lifetime down here and never see one, and if I had thought about it, if I had done something besides just stand on the bridge-wing and look at it, I might have known...."

"You might have known what?" I said because I had just about convinced myself that there really was something wrong with him, back then had unsettled him, set him off center, for who could believe that something in the sky would follow a ship on the ocean?

"I might have heard it was howling, 'Get ready everyone,' that it was growling there were plenty of strange things on the ocean and this was just a sample because, and listen to me, I was absolutely sure that thing wasn't following the ship...I was sure it was following me."

He was silent and I was, he with the memory of seeing something I would never see and me, terrified that one could be around us, even in the night.

"Do they come in the dark?" I said to him.

"Who knows when they come," he said and turned to face me, looked in what light there was from the moon. He wanted to see my face again.

"I'm no more easily frightened than the next man," he said. "Do you believe that?"

"I believe it."

"It takes a lot to frighten a man, even more when there are other men around."

"And even more than that if there are women."

"Yes," he said, "of course. Then most of all."

"And what happened?" I said.

"To what?"

He had forgotten. He had gone off some-place again, for she was still there, nowhere I knew but I would.

"The waterspout," I said, "the tornado, that thing you saw in the sky."

He was still looking at me and then he turned away. I wondered if he had seen what he wanted in my face.

"We ran right at it," he said. "Finally, when it was only a half-mile away we went right at it and when we got closer it went across the bows to the north-west. Maybe it had wasted enough time and was back on course to wherever it was going. We turned back for Bimini again and I watched the thing on the radar. It went off the five-mile range, the ten- mile, and then I couldn't see it on the twenty- mile scale. It was gone."

Where did it go? I thought to myself. Where do they go and where do they come from, and why? I was going to ask him but he was almost at the end.

"I would have steamed around forever rather than go right at that thing, but that's what the Captain did. Sometimes on a collision course one thing to do is run right at the other ship and you lose the collision angle, but I wouldn't have done it."

"I never did it when I had the underweigh watch. If I was on a collision course with another ship, and we were on plenty with those fifteen-hundred foot tankers running up and down the Gulf Stream, I turned ninety degrees away, what most people do. If the Captain had ever missed the ship it might have gone someplace with me, but not straight at that tornado."

"And it was an omen?" I said and tried to see into the dark on the water, looked to see again if one was there, but he didn't hear me.

"If we had gotten any closer that thing might have gibbered, it might have whispered we were crazy, too, crazy to be out there on anything as big as an ocean, insane to think we could rescue anything at all. And then everyone went back about their business."

"The Captain had run right at it and it was gone. I didn't think anymore about it. I thought about it later all right, more than once, and even saw it again down in the wardroom when the bowl on the table began to move. I remembered how it followed, ...how I knew it followed me."

"A demon" I said and thought a demon could look like that if there were such things as demons.

"Someone like that," he said, "or the brother of one."

V

"The Captain," I said, what was he like?"

"He was a mustang."

"That's some kind of horse."

"It's an expression, someone who starts out as a seaman and makes first-class or Chief, then becomes an officer and starts at the bottom again. He was a Lieutenant Commander when I knew him, Lieutenant Commander Richard D. Tibbetts, USCG."

"And he steered at tornadoes?"

"It was the thing to do. We were nervous, everybody on the bridge was, and that was the thing to do. They called him, 'Long-Head' on the ship, not when he was around, but that's what they called him. Do mules have long heads?"

"I never saw a mule."

He had his hands in his pockets again and

was looking down at the sand between his feet.

"If you saw him in the street you'd have thought he ran a drugstore if you thought anything about him at all. He looked just like everybody else except that his hair was cut short, that and his hands. "

"What about his hands?"

"One hand. He'd done something to it down on a deck somewhere when he was first in the service. Two of the fingers were stiff and he couldn't close them into a fist. When he was drinking a mug of coffee they stuck out like somebody drinking tea"

He took one hand out of his pocket and opened and closed the fingers, closing them into a fist and opening them.

"But those fingers didn't get in his way and he didn't learn about tornadoes up in Officer Candidate's School. What he knew he learned bending over and picking it up one piece at a time, the way you'd pick up a length of line lying on the deck and put it away. It was all in his head the way our gunner's mate stored ordnance, so you could put your hand right on it in the dark. When things would go wrong, and they did sometimes, he would light up that pipe of his and say to me, 'It's got two ends, Mr. Farrington,' and we'd go at it."

"We got along, too, a whole lot better than some CO's and XO's I knew. He liked the way all the paper was done and he used to talk about how I ought to make a career in the Coast Guard and have a ship of my own, stay in twenty or twenty-five years and make a name for myself."

"But it was the Captain, he and the Chief Bosun, the engineer and the first-class quartermaster who ran the ship when we really had something to do, all one-hundred and twenty-five feet of her and nearly forty of us. We sailed around all over the place towing broken-down yachts, dragging grounded boats off sandbars, looking for yachtsmen who weren't even out on the water. They were in somebody's bed and only their wives thought they were lost."

"We searched, you wouldn't believe the searching we did, day after day of it, but somebody else always had the rescue, a helicopter out of Miami, a forty-footer, or the 255' they keep down there for the big ones, and I'll tell you something,"

"What?"

"More than anything else I wanted to be in a rescue, a part of one anyway. I know what that sounds like and you can think what you want, but you would have felt the same, any man would."

I wondered if I would, if a long time ago I would have wanted to rescue someone in the sea.

"I suppose anyone would," I said.

"Of course they would," he said, "and all that I said about not being sure on the ship, that changed. By the time I had been on there for four years damned near every day, Saturdays, Sundays, holidays, seen everything done and done most of it myself, after a while I knew what I was doing. And all we did was to go from one end of Florida to the other, out into the Bahamas, down to Cuba, around the corner and into the Gulf of Mexico and never rescued a single person."

"I wanted to rescue somebody, wanted the ship with me on it to do that. Christ, we were a search and rescue vessel and all we ever did was search."

He had been talking a long time, the way a person will who hasn't except for a word here and there to keep a day going. He hadn't come any closer to that place on the water sixty miles away. He was going around and around it still standing in the same place, his feet a yard away from the water.

And then he said,

"If I'd been lucky that's all we'd have done."

"What did you say?"

He was looking out across the water, still taking some bearing in his mind.

"I said search. If all we'd ever done was that, we would never have found anything. We could have just kept on doing it, stand watches, sleep, eat and stand watches again, write it all down in the log, and go home. We only had to do it for a few more months and I would have been...."

"What?" I said, again. It seemed like all I could say. It sounded like a bird. It might have been a bird in one of those trees behind us sitting on a limb in the dark.

"Safe," he said and there was a sound out on the water in front of us.

"What was that?"

"Anything, barracuda, ray, shark, they're everywhere out there at night."

"Everywhere?"

"At night they are."

"How do you know?"

"I've heard them before, plenty of times. You don't serve down here for four years without hearing that."

I moved away from the water, back toward the shadow of the trees where maybe there were birds, but there weren't any birds. There was only me saying, 'What?' If there were any birds they had gone someplace else or to sleep. Everything was gone or asleep except the two of us standing on the sand with something in the water in front of us.

And then the sound came again.

It was much louder, a crash as if somebody had dropped some heavy thing on the water or sent it up into the air so you could hear it come down again and that was all. In the silver from the moon we saw nothing, heard not another sound. It was eerie and not something I liked to hear and I wanted him to talk again, to say something, so I said,

"Were there just the two of you?"

"Of course" he said. He was still standing near the water, his back to me, only a blacker place in the dark.

"That must have been difficult," I said, only the two of you."

"What do you mean?" he said. "There was nothing difficult about it. Once I had made up my mind it was the right thing to do, I just told her all there was to tell."

The girl, the woman, had come back, if she had ever gone. He raised his hand again the way he had before only this time it was as if she was in a swing, had swung a long way away, and come back.

But I had made a mistake.

"I meant you and the Captain," I said. "Were you the only officers?"

He didn't answer, and when he did I

could barely hear him.

"No," he said and I walked back and stood beside him.

"There were three of us," he said.

"Who was the other one?"

But something had happened to him. I could feel it in the way he stood. He was just as he had been when we first met, standing in the road, off-center but like a rock in the dark.

"An ensign," he said, "Ensign John Gregory."

"Just the three of you?"

"The three of us and a Warrant Engineer, a first-class quartermaster, and the crew. Ensign John Gregory, United States Coast Guard Academy, was our Deck Officer."

"The Academy, was it like Annapolis?"

"And West Point, all the same drill, four years of it along with the summers."

"What was wrong with him?" I said

"What do you mean?" and he turned to

me.

"You sound like there was something. It was in the way you said his name."

He laughed then and slapped me on the shoulder.

"There was something wrong with him all right – or something right – the day he came up that gangway with the visor of his cap like a mirror and his orders under his arm. He had hair that color inside an ear of corn and blue eyes and I wondered if I could ever have looked as young as that. With those two blue eyes to go with the two gold bars on his collars he looked like he came out of a box."

"And I was standing there at the head of the gangway in washed-out khakis, dried-out shoes, with the visor of my hat as green as dirty brass. He threw a salute that came out of a cannon and said, 'Ensign John Gregory, reporting for duty, sir.'"

"And that's what he'd come for, too, —

duty. He'd had four years plus of the same things I'd had four months of and he wasn't aboard just because there was a war on. He'd come to stay, the route, and it made a difference."

"Did you get along?"

"Right up until nearly the end we did, until I had to make him tell me why he did it. You couldn't make friends on the ship, not with the crew anyway. Officers weren't supposed to fraternize, and not with the Captain, either. You don't make friends with the Captain if you're one of his officers."

"John and I got along all right even if everybody knew Academy men didn't think much of hundred and twenty day wonders. We talked when we were off watch down in the wardroom and the first-class quartermaster had the underweigh duty. We even had a couple of liberties together but all he ever wanted to talk about was the ship and the Captain. He wanted to know everything I knew about the Captain. The one thing he really wanted to know he didn't talk about and neither did I."

"What was that?"

"How he would be."

"How he would be?"

"How you're going to act when it happens," he said, "when you have to do what you've been paid to do all along and never done, and I don't mean towing yachts around or pulling them off sandbars."

"What do you mean?" I said and he was very close to me now.

"I mean when you have to pull somebody out of an ocean and things have gone out of control."

He turned then and walked toward the trees, not far, and sat down in the sand.

"Why don't you sit down?" he said, "there's more to this," and he laughed again, the better laugh, but not the one I wished to hear.

I walked to where he was and sat in the sand, fine white sand still warm from a sun that was shining somewhere, and there was more, how much more I could not have guessed.

"Ensign John Gregory was a career man," he said, "Just started in on thirty years and I remember wondering if he would ever make it. He wasn't very big and had white skin with freckles on his hands and that yellow hair, yellow as a stop sign. When we were out on patrol he sunburned his nose and it always had that white salve on it. His nose peeled the whole time and he was always feeling it to see if it was still there. I'll tell you he didn't look like he could last thirty years."

"But he was an Academy man. You could tell that just by the way he walked. It's supposed to make a difference, and it does, some kind of a difference anyway."

"He stood up straight even when he was sitting down and it drove me crazy watching him eat. And there were too many 'sirs' when he was around the Captain, too. You didn't have to 'sir' the Captain. I never did anyway and I got along with him better than John. The Captain and I talked when we had the chance, and not just about the ship, either. He was always telling me how fine I would feel when I had settled down and had my future in hand. That was what he said, '…when I had my future in hand.'"

Both of his hands were in front of him in something like a bowl. He was looking at them, at least it seemed that way in the light from the moon. But with his head down the way it was he could have had is eyes closed and be seeing something I could not see at all.

"The hull held us up, the compass pointed where we were going, and we did what the Captain told us to do and why not? He knew more about what we were supposed to be doing than anyone else. He was just the damned Captain, wasn't he? But that wasn't what John thought. Even though he was a mustang and up through the ranks, with a couple of stiff fingers and stubborn as a mule, John was looking for something else. He was right, too, about that. I didn't know it then, but he was. The Captain was another kind of man."

Were there really other kind of men, I thought? There were different men, there were already three different kinds of men on that ship, one with two stiff fingers, one with corn-colored hair and one who stood in the road in the dark, but was one of them another kind altogether? If he was he was a kind I had never met.

"John was good at what he had to do. And he had the Chief Bosun the same as I did when I'd come aboard. The Captain spent most of his time in his cabin when we were underweigh. He didn't stand watches, but if it was night, if it was the middle of the night and some thirteen-hundred foot tanker was running down the Straights on automatic pilot, five hundred thousand deadweight tons with maybe somebody on the bridge and maybe not, he was behind you in the dark. You didn't have to call him and say you had to make a course change. You could smell that pipe and see the white mug on the chart table because he was there before you could press the button on the phone."

"We stood plenty of watches on that ship, John and I and the quartermaster, four on and eight off, running three or four hundred miles out to find somebody who had forgotten to fill his fuel tanks before he left Nassau or some Sunday driver who broke down in the Northwest Providence Channel. We went and found them and towed them in and if it wasn't much fun on the end of a towline with a sea running, it wasn't our fault. We brought them in, dropped the line, and went back out for another one. It's a miracle they don't all drown out there. Something takes care of them - not us - but something."

"Except once," I said.

"Yes, except once."

And there was silence, no sound at all from the sea or the sky or the dark trees behind us. It was as if we were waiting for something, a tap on the podium from the black dome above us, because we were finally there.

The girl, the ship, the Captain, even the sea in front of us scrolled by the wind were overture. Somewhere out there to the northwest another man who had no friend had not known his enemy.

PART TWO

I

"Those small boats came out through the Bimini Channel one behind the other and there were boats spread out all around us, up to the north and down to the south. In that bay as clear as tonic water they'd had their convention or reunion or party with plenty of rum, safe from waterspouts and wives, but they were late. Half of them hadn't made the departure time but the sun was up in a blue sky, fifteen or twenty mile visibility, and no sea. What there was of a wind couldn't have been three knots from the south-east and I was up on the flying-bridge counting."

"Twenty-two, twenty-three, twenty-four small boats around us like ducks on a pond. They were all there, finally, and if the weather held up and nobody broke down, we'd be home by dark."

"John had the watch down on the bridge-wing and he was counting, too. He counted the boats to starboard and then walked through the bridge and counted them to port. The Captain was leaning on the railing and he looked up at me. I held out two fingers on my left hand and four on my right and he nodded, turned to John, and I felt the ship move west, straight out into the Gulf Stream."

"It was 'Baker's Watch', three of the engineers down in the engine room; quartermaster, radioman, and a seaman on the bridge, look-out up above, the cook and the mess boy down in the galley. Back on the fantail you could see Malloy, our Gunner's Mate, painting the depth-charge racks. What armament we had was Malloy's, the forty-millimeter forward, a twenty-millimeter on top of the deckhouse, and back on the fantail two lines of depth charges on their racks. It was old gear, left over from another war and ready to be deep-sixed in a thousand fathoms."

"But Malloy thought every day there would be a war to go to and the Coast Guard Cutter Travis would sail out after submarines with the old forty-millimeter firing ten rounds a minute if it didn't jam, the twenty sticking a finger into the sky, and astern of us the ocean would explode if the depth charges still worked."

"That ship would never go to another war. She'd been passed by, or over, and to watch her waddle across the Stream you'd think she ought to be saving herself instead of hobbling around the ocean trying to save somebody else. Just three months ago down in the bilge one of the engineers put a chipping hammer through her bottom. The plates were gone they said, but they only hauled us and welded on another one like a band-aid. The Bosun called her a 'slow-goer' and she was, too old and too slow, and I just wanted to save somebody before they towed her away."

"Three times every day Malloy took temperatures down in the magazine and he washed his hands before he crawled in there, too. Temperatures of the forty and twenty-millimeter shells, the thirty and forty-five caliber ammunition like they were sick kids that lived down there in wooden crates. Malloy was ready and the ship was as ready as a thirty-five year old ship could be. The loran put us somewhere in Africa but the radar worked; the gyro quit when it felt like it but the magnetic compass was fine if you didn't have change in your pocket, and the diesels would run until she died. There were eyes and hands and plenty of line and maybe we could rescue somebody if anyone would give us a chance."

"I climbed down the ladder to the deck and went below to the galley. Henry was in there, along with the mess-cook, and he smiled the way he always did even with six inches of water on the galley deck and a roast beef banging back and forth in the oven,"

"'Roast pork, black-eyed peas, lime jello, Mr. Farrington,' "he said, and I hoped the sea would stay calm. Inside the big refrigerator I cut myself a piece of baloney, put it in bread, and went into the wardroom. There was nobody there, the Captain and John were up on the bridge, and I sat down at the wardroom table. It was right there at that table where it began and maybe that was where it ended, too."

"At a table?" I said.

"Around a table," he smiled, "that wasn't

round. It was where it began, anyway, where you found out where you had to go and what you needed to get there."

'Anyway' was the right word, I thought. People didn't sit around round tables and decide to save somebody, not anymore, not this side of King Arthur, anyway.

"There was green felt on the table and a sugar bowl sitting in the middle. Down underneath I could hear the diesels running, the generator, the hum of the converter spinning around so that up on the mast the radar antenna could turn and the big potato masher Henry had in the galley could mash. The shafts revolved and spun the propellers beating away under the water, driving all those men and machinery and a roast pork with black-eyed peas across an ocean. I watched the white sugar bowl shake in the sound, a round white haze on the green felt."

"The night before I had the anchor watch,

the mid, from twelve to four and I closed my eyes in the humming and floated in the sound, leaning back against the hull of the ship. The last thing I saw was the sugar bowl. Its edges blurred, a round grayness on the table top."

"And then it grew, climbed until it was the waterspout up in a quarter of the sky. I was asleep, in a dream, but I remember it so well it could be here right now, right there," and he pointed at some place out on the dark water in front of us."

I jumped. There were things on top of the water and under it and we were not a dozen feet away. I put both of my hands down on the sand, one on each side of me and felt it with my fingers.

"And I fell asleep with half a baloney sandwich in my hand. How much time went by, how long that funnel tracked me, I don't know. An hour, maybe two, I ran up hills and into hollows running nowhere, a dry horizon in front of me like a pencil line. The sweat came out under my arms and down my back, and then I fell into a hole and up above me I could see that gray thing in the sky. It was like a sinew or the long neck of a bird without skin or a head and only a hole at the top. I tried to get up, to climb out and pushed with my feet against the deck and my shoulders against the bulkhead but I couldn't move, and then I woke up and had to hold myself against the motion of the ship."

"The sugar bowl was sliding, three or four inches one way on the green table and it stopped. Then it went the other way. It slid toward me and ran to the edge and I caught it just before it went over."

"The inclinometer hung on the bulkhead of the wardroom and the pointer swung fifteen degrees left until it stopped — back through zero — and up to fifteen on the other side. It was as steady as a clock.

They'd come up fast, I thought, long ones from somewhere and it didn't feel like they were going to stop. The buzzer on the bridge phone went off and I tried to stand up, jammed my knee against the table, and took the phone off the hook,"

"'Wardroom,' "I said."

"'The Captain wants you on the bridge, sir,' "it was the duty quartermaster."

"'Weather?'"

"'Message from the District, Mr. Farrington, weather advisory. The Captain wants you on the bridge,' and he hung up."

"I got out from behind the table, through the hatch into the passage

way, up a ladder, along another passageway, out through another hatch onto the deck and the sea had changed. The sun was gone and I climbed the ladder to the bridge."

"The Captain and John were bent over the chart table and the seaman at the wheel looked at me, half a look to make sure we were all there. Through the door to the radio room I could hear Collins banging away on the Morse key. All the lights on the big transmitter were burning and Rowling, the quartermaster, was jammed in a corner of the bridge holding himself there with his shoulders."

"'There's a message from the District, Francis,' the Captain said and for the first time since I'd been on that ship there was something different about him. He didn't look the same for one thing. There was no pipe, no mug of coffee and he handed me the message and waited, stood there looking at me and waiting."

"What was he waiting for?" I said. Now I had my hands around my knees pulled up tight like a ball.

"I don't know. I didn't know then and I still don't. Maybe he was looking for a sign. Maybe he was looking so far ahead...."

How far ahead can you see, I thought? It must be pretty far if you know what you're looking for, if you can see it far down the road, in the middle of all those things that haven't happened yet.

"The message looked the same as a hundred others, all in capital letters, typed on Collins' old machine. Some of the letters didn't work and the slant-bar wrote a question mark, but you could read them if you'd read enough."

"It wasn't the same, though, because the message was just for us, not for 'ALL UNITS SEVENTH COAST GUARD DISTRICT,' not even to all search and rescue vessels. It was just to us, CGC Travis (WSC 153),"

> 3716?081410?01
> TO: CGC TRAVIS, WSC 153
> FROM: COMMANDER
> SEVENTH COAST GUARD

DISTRICT
TEXT: URGENT WEATHER.
CGC AIR STATION MIAMI
ADVISES LINE SQUALLS YOUR
AREA IMMINENT.

"I read it again because 'urgent' wasn't a word you heard very often in a message out of Miami. I handed it back to the Captain and I said,"

" 'I haven't seen them use 'urgent' before'."

"He was still just standing there watching me read the message. He took the flimsy yellow paper and said to me,"

" 'I haven't either, Francis, not ever,' and turned and went into the radio room."

"Out on the bridge-wing there was no wind at all. The sea was up with swells coming from somewhere, gray as gun barrels, but the color of the sky was wrong. It was rose as if something was on fire behind it, and there were no clouds. Even down at the horizon there were no clouds, only a haze in the rose-colored sky."

"John came out on the bridge-wing beside me and said,"

"'How bad can they get?' "but I didn't answer him. I was looking at the sky and I felt cold. I was sweating again."

"'What's that in your hand?' John said and I looked. It was what was left of the sandwich, the one I was eating in the wardroom."

"'Nothing,' I said and threw it over the side. I watched it float down the wake. I was waiting for a gull to take it but there weren't any gulls."

"'Francis,' the Captain spoke from inside the bridge."

"'Call the small boats and tell them thirty to forty knots of wind from the south-east,' he said, 'tell them it will be any time now.'"

"It was hot inside the radio room, even

with the ventilators in the overhead, hot
from the transmitters and receivers. Collins
was sending something and he swung
around in his swivel chair and rolled a message form into the typewriter. Through the
door to the radio room I could see John and
the quartermaster looking out through the
port hatch. All the small boats were on that
side to the south of us and the Captain was
on the other side, looking out through the
starboard hatch."

"There was nothing for him to see. There
was nothing but empty ocean stretching
away to the north with the Gulf Stream
under it all the way to Labrador."

"The transceiver was on the port bulkhead. It was just a gray box with dials and
switches and a microphone hanging from a
hook. I turned the knob to 2182 and keyed
the button on the microphone. The red
light came on."

"'Coast Guard Cutter Travis to all small

boats,' I said, 'weather advisory follows.'"

"As I spoke the needle on the dial moved with my voice and out there they heard me."

"Under a rose-colored sky with no clouds," I said.

"Yes."

"Isn't that strange?"

"It is. It was the strangest thing I had ever seen."

"Stranger than the waterspout?"

"Yes, because it was all around you and because the color was wrong. It was what you might want to find in a woman's bedroom."

I tried to remember it, to see the flush again and hold it in my mind, but he went on.

"I told the small boats what the message said,"

"'Line squalls imminent. Force six to seven,' and I said it again, and a third time,' and reached for the 'off' switch' but Collins said,"

"'Better leave that on, Mr. Farrington,' and he handed me another message."

"Down in Search and Rescue in Miami they were looking at this big wall chart of the Seventh Coast Guard District, Cuba to Georgia. And we were on it, on the chart, a marker saying, 'CGC Travis (WSC 153). We were on the Status Board, too: 'TRAVIS – Escort Duty – twenty-four (24) Small Boats – Bimini - Lauderdale.' They were worried in Miami but not about us."

3716?081440?02
FROM: COMMANDER SEVENTH
COAST GUARD DISTRICT
TO: CGC TRAVIS (WSC 153)
TEXT: URGENT WEATHER. CG
AIR STATION MIAMI ADVISES
VERY SEVERE SQUALLS FORCE
TEN PLUS YOUR AREA

IMMINENT.

"It sounded like the same message all over again but it wasn't. Out on the bridge I gave it to the Captain and waited for him to say something. He read it, leaned over the chart table, and walked a pair of dividers up the chart to the north."

"What shall I tell them, Captain?' I said."

"Repeat the weather every fifteen minutes, Francis, and tell them sixty knots of wind.'"

I knew what rose-colored was, a blush or a flush, and could see his sky, but I didn't know a knot. I had wanted to ask him the first time and now I did. It was a stupid question, something you ought to know, anybody ought to, but almost no one does. Like how far it is to the nearest star or how much does water weigh?

"Would you tell me what a knot is?"

"It's one nautical mile an hour."

"And a nautical mile?"

"Two thousand yards."

"Francis," I said, "how much is sixty knots of wind?"

In the middle of numbers and asking a stupid question, it was the first time I had called him by his name.

"Seventy miles an hour," he said, like a parenthesis. He was far into his story and interruptions meant nothing to him.

"Then the Captain turned to Rowling and said,"

"'We'll need that log, Rowling, of current variations,' and he looked at the quarter-master, too, the way he had looked at me."

"Then he turned to John."

"'Call the Bosun to the bridge, Mr. Gregory,' he said and now he had looked at the three of us." "I wondered what he had seen or what he had been looking for. We were the underweigh watch officers, the three who conned the ship at night when two-thirds of the crew were asleep below in their bunks. Maybe John and Rowling knew what the Captain was looking for but I didn't, not then I didn't."

Then he said,

"Have you ever had the feeling that everyone knew something you didn't know?"

It was a feeling I knew well, but I knew, too, that it was only a feeling and not true, as if there was a conspiracy behind the hands people held before their mouths.

"Yes," I said, "I've had that feeling, but they don't."

"Don't what?"

"They don't know something you don't know."

He looked at me and even in the moonlight it was the oddest expression, as if he knew I was wrong but wanted me to be right, that if I was right made a difference.

"The feeling was there, though, just the same," he said, "something the Captain knew and the other two might have guessed. It was like everybody else had finished reading the book and you had only started, and then the loudspeakers went on."

"'Bosun to the bridge — Bosun to the bridge,' and it sounded down in the galley, the crew's quarters, in the cabins. The port hatch opened and the Bosun stepped over the combing."

"Chief Petty Officer Warren Minzy had been on the ship as long as anyone could remember. He was part of it, like the deck or the hull, tall and thin with a face like a knot in wood. If he drank too much ashore, he did everything you asked him to aboard, and some things you didn't, but he held the ship together, him and a thousand coats of paint."

"'Bosun on the bridge, sir.'"

"'There's going to be some wind,' the Captain said and he still had the pair of dividers in his good hand. They were open two or three inches and I had the crazy thought that if I knew what those two or three inches meant, what he had measured with them, I'd know what everybody else already knew."

"'And when it's over there'll be things to do,' the Captain said. 'I want the fifteen-man inflatable for the fore-castle, heaving lines, stokes litter and three-quarter inch nylon.'"

"'Yes, sir.'"

"'And everybody in life jackets.'"

The Bosun nodded and then he nodded at everybody on the bridge, at me and Rowling and John, and went out through the hatch."

"John was standing by the engine-order telegraph with his hands on the handles. They were high polished brass and he held them in his white hands and looked out through one of the forward port-holes, over the fore-castle, the bow, out into the sea ahead of us."

"'Can the small boats take sixty knots of wind?' he said."

"'Some of them won't,' the Captain said and he looked over at me. He had this expression on his face that was nearly a smile and he said,

"'But that's what we're here for, isn't it?'"

"It was what we were there for all right but I had never heard anyone say it before. What seemed like a long time ago I had thought it but had forgotten. In that routine we had every day you'd forget anything. But yes, I wanted to be in a rescue, a real one, and I still didn't think it would ever happen."

"And it did?" I said.

"Yes."

"The kind of rescue you wanted?"

He didn't say anything to that. He only sat with his hands between his legs, and finally,

"No," he said, "you couldn't say that."

But he had said it before, back when we had first met and were sitting at the table drinking cognac. He had said exactly the same thing when I had asked him, 'You come here just to get away from it all,' and he had said, 'No, you couldn't say that.'

"Well, what kind was it if it wasn't the kind you wanted? A rescue's a rescue, isn't it?"

He wouldn't answer. It was infuriating the way he just sat there and ignored everything I said. He was like some kind of train running on tracks. He stopped now and then, at stations, but then he just kept on going.

"Just the same, though, on that bridge something was going on that had not happened before."

And he was off again.

"I want Malloy, too,' the Captain said

and I went to the PA."

"'Gunner's Mate Malloy to the bridge!' I said and I said it too loud and the speakers screeched but before I could say it again, Malloy came through the starboard hatch."

"'Gunner's Mate Malloy reporting, sir,' he said straight as a cleaning rod, dressed in those whites, the only man aboard who wore them every day. He was unique on board that ship. You could see him up on the forecastle lubricating the recoil mechanism on the 40 millimeter cannon, in his white uniform with an apron on."

"'Line-throwing gun and the big flares, Malloy,' the Captain said."

"'Yes, sir,' and he snapped a salute and was gone."

"'Rowling?' the Captain said."

"'Yes, sir.'"

"'The searchlight?'"

"'All right for looking, sir, no good for signaling. The shutter's broke.'"

"'We won't be signaling,' the Captain said, 'and a helmsman?'"

"'Stone, sir, quartermaster striker Stone.'"

"'We'll want him,' the Captain said and went back to the chart table and started walking those dividers up and down the chart again."

"I looked at the clock next to the wind speed indicator. It said eleven o'clock. Eleven o'clock in the morning with a rose-colored sky and the Captain was talking about flares and searchlights. And it felt like people were moving all over the ship, the crew opening compartments, dragging out gear, closing hatches. The sea was up but there was no wind. The indicator was at zero and it was getting warmer, no wind and warmer."

"'Reduce speed, Mr. Gregory,' the Captain said, 'make five knots.'"

"John rang the handles on the engine-order telegraph down and back and bells jangled down below. He spoke into the sound-powered telephone,"

"'Engine room – Bridge. Make five knots,' and the sound of the engines throttled down until you could just hear them, feel them both up through the steel of the ship and the bottoms of your feet."

"The Captain called the three of us over to the chart table and we all looked down at Coast and Geodetic 20176. It doesn't seem possible that it could all happen on there. If we had that piece of paper here right now nearly everything would be on it."

"Nearly everything?" I said.

He drew a rectangle in the sand. Four straight lines with sand inside them.

"No, not everything," he said, "but I can tell you more than once I thought about it lying there on the chart table, four or five square feet of paper with numbers and lines drawn on it."

He dropped his head so I couldn't see his

face.

"Are you tired?" I said.

"No, I'm not tired." He ran his hand back and forth across the sand and erased the lines he had drawn.

"I wonder," he said, "I still wonder...."

"What?"

"Whether she understood it. Whether a woman could have understood."

"A woman can understand anything, they say."

"Can they?"

"They must," I said, never having known whether they did or not.

"She was not just any kind of woman."

"I believe you."

"She would have had to . . .."

"Understand?"

"Yes."

"About the man you rescued."

"No, not the man we rescued," and he drew the rectangle in the sand again.

"The one we lost," he said and wiped the lines away.

II

"On the chart the land was colored yellow and the sea was blue, dark blue where the deep water was and light blue everywhere else. Rowling had drawn a pencil line from Bimini to Fort Lauderdale with times and crosses on it like beads on a string. Half-way across he'd written, '281 degrees true,' the course you had to steer to make Lauderdale with the Gulf Stream under you and there wasn't a sound on the bridge, nothing but the ship moving through the ocean until the Captain said,"

"'It will be anytime now."

"John was still staring down at the chart and I went over and looked at it again. It was the same. Everything on the bridge was different but that chart was the same: depths, types of bottom, shoaling over the

Grand Bahama Bank, Bimini no bigger
than a carpet tack, and the mainland, half
the state of Florida hanging down from the
north like a big thumb."

"John had both hands flat on the table,
leaning over it, and I tried to see whatever
the hell it was he saw, looked at a chart I
had looked at a thousand times before, and
saw nothing."

"'When the wind comes,' the Captain
said, 'we're going to lose one or two of
those boats.'"

"The Captain was talking about something that hadn't happened yet, that maybe
wouldn't happen if whatever was coming
never came. I felt the sweat start down the
middle of my back. Not a thing had happened and already I was sweating and I
said,"

"'We could do something...before it
comes.'"

"'There's nothing we can do now,' he said

and walked out on the wing of the bridge."

"The rose color was inside now. It filled the bridge with pink. Everybody looked like they were powdered and painted like in one of those plays where everybody wears wigs and then a buzzer went off,"

"'Bridge!'"

"It came out of the voice tube from the flying-bridge above us."

"'Small boat signaling, port bow, two-hundred yards,' the look-out called and John went out on the bridge-wing."

"It was his watch and he braced himself against the railing and brought the binoculars up to his eyes. There was a real swell running now and he was having trouble keeping his feet without holding on."

"Then the ship rolled hard. The helmsman started to slide on the deck and caught himself with one hand before he went down. He had one hand on the wheel and one on the magnetic compass and he looked at

Rowling, afraid to look the other way and see the Captain."

"'Watch that,' Rowling said and the man brought the ship back on but with too much rudder and we rolled the other way."

"He didn't like it, that helmsman, any of it, the color of the sky, what he had heard on the bridge, the way the big seas came at him from off the port bow and lifted the ship, that least of all."

"'Small boat signaling, Captain,' John said. "'They're waving something white.'"

"'Take us over there, but not too close. Stay downwind of them. Francis, use the loud-hailer.'"

"'Come left, steer 270,' John said and the helmsman spun the wheel over, too far, and we drove into a wave. There was white water on the fore-castle and everyone held on with both hands, and then we were back, rolling, with the inclinometer on the bulkhead reading twenty-five degrees of roll."

"'Steer 270,' John said and the helmsman started to say something and couldn't, opened his mouth and tried to speak with three officers and a first-class quartermaster on the bridge and couldn't."

"I went out on the bridge-wing with the microphone in my hand. There were two men in the boat crouched down in the stern with foul weather gear and hoods. They had orange life jackets on with the collars up and they looked like two kids ready to go out and play."

"Their boat was only just climbing the waves, up and then up more, then down into the trough with the seas above them, and there was still no wind."

"One of them was waving a wooden pole with something on the end of it. It looked like a head, a white one, with long, stringy hair, and then I saw what it was. A mop. It was a white cotton mop on the end of a pole."

"'ABOARD THE SMALL BOAT,' I said into the microphone and from the speaker above me on the flying-bridge I heard my voice bellow. It didn't sound like me. It didn't sound like anybody I had ever heard before."

"That voice that came out of the bullhorn wasn't me. It was somebody with a pink face holding on with one hand, a leg through the railing, trying to talk to a man with a mop."

"They said something down in the boat, first one of the men and then the other, and the one with the mop was still waving it, forward and back, waving us closer."

"'ARE YOU IN TROUBLE?' I boomed across the water."

"The man with the mop nodded his head but the other man shook his and cupped his hands around his mouth,"

"'...take us aboard?' he yelled and the other one nodded his head faster."

"'Did you hear him, Captain?' I said."

He was standing on the bridge-wing holding onto the railing with one hand and shaking his head,"

"'Too much sea,' he said. 'It will take too long. If we stop now we'll fall behind the others.'"

"I turned to the small boat rising on a sea twenty yards from us,"

"'TOO MUCH SEA...HAVE TO STAY WITH THE OTHERS,' and I saw the man with the mop turn to the other. I knew what he was saying. He was saying they were one of the 'others', but the man at the wheel shook his head again, looked up at us, and waved."

"'Come back on course,' the Captain said.'"

"And we turned away from the small boat. I watched them wallowing in the swells. Whatever was coming was coming to them, too, and they'd have a story to tell at a dinner party or in a bar, after it was over. The man with the mop was still holding it up in the air, but he wasn't waving. He was just holding it between his feet and in both hands like a flag of defeat. They'd have a story to tell after it was over all right, if they were there when it was."

"On the bridge I looked at the clock. It was ten minutes to twelve. It was my watch."

"'I relieve you,' I said to John."

"'Course 281 degrees true, speed five knots,' he said."

"I nodded and we looked at each other then the way you look at whoever's next to you in a race. More than once later on I wondered what he thought when we stood there. I wondered if he could have already made up his mind? I would have given a lot to have known that, even afterwards."

"The whole watch was being relieved, the helmsman, the quartermaster, the look-out, and the helmsman was ready for relief. Four hours of trying to steer, trying to hold on, staring at the compass and not wanting to look out at the seas. He needed relief but it didn't come quick enough and he was sick."

"He'd held it to as near twelve o'clock as he could and he couldn't anymore, vomited on the wheel, on himself, a puddle of it on the deck between his feet. And that's something you don't do on a bridge, ever."

"Rowling got him out of there, had the deck cleaned up, the wheel swabbed, but I saw the helmsman's face. It was flat white like an undercoat of paint. Not at what he had done, he didn't look like he knew what he had done. He just looked scared."

"Scared of what he had heard in those messages from Miami Air Station and wishing to God he was somewhere else, anywhere else except where he was on a ship with plenty of places to hide but with something coming you couldn't hide from."

"I got the new helmsman on course and started the entry in the rough log and thought maybe the sky would just get redder and redder until we were home, and then it would come, after we were in port with the bow and stern lines, the spring lines, the shore-power cable, the water hose and the telephone hooked up to the dock and then it could do anything it wanted. And I'll tell you honestly I don't know if I wanted it to come or not."

And to tell the truth, I didn't know myself. Something terrible was going to happen, maybe to him, certainly to somebody, and I thought for a moment about whether it did any good to tell people about the terrible things that can happen. Are people better off not knowing about things that could never happen to them, things about which they could have done nothing when they happened and about which they can do nothing now?

"Are you sure you want to go on with this?" I said.

He got up and walked back to where he had been before, six feet or so from the sea. I could hear him even with his back turned.

"Of course," he said. "You have to go to the end, don't you?"

I guess you do, I thought. I guess that is what you have to do and so I said,

"Yes."

And he went on.

"I told you that feeling on the bridge was nothing like it had always been because now people were looking at each other as if they didn't know or weren't sure who you were, people who had known each other for months, even years. The Captain said we would lose some of the boats and that meant we would have to try to save somebody. And I didn't know if you could save anybody in the seas he said were coming."

"How would you get close enough, and if you did, how would you get them aboard? If you got too close you'd kill them and if there were men in the water you couldn't get them up the steel sides of a ship rolling in twenty foot seas. I didn't know if you could do any of it and standing in that pink light I didn't know if I wanted to, and then it started to get colder."

"It was as if someone had opened the door of a cold storage room where they hang meat. In seconds it was cold, and getting colder, and Rowling said,"

"'Off to port, Mr. Farrington,' he said, '...the squall line.'"

"On the bridge-wing it was like winter, one of those mornings with no wind and frost, and when I looked across the sea to port it was something to take your breath away. Out there, in a line along the horizon, was a wall."

A shiver went through me. I got up,

thought better of it, and sat back down.

"It was long and gray, black in places like the bands people wear around their arms, like some kind of curtain rising from the bottom of the sky, and it had come from nowhere. It hadn't been there five minutes ago, I know, I was looking, everywhere around us but there had been nothing, nothing except the red sky and the sea."

"Somewhere down below the horizon it had spread itself into that wall and come up over the edge of the world. In the bottom of my stomach I had the feeling of ice under a car going too fast because the wall was moving toward us, an ash-colored wall black at the bottom and flecks of white as if it was pushing something in front of it."

"I went back on the bridge and put my hands under my arms. My hands were cold, the way they were when I had to go into the big freezer down in the galley. Once a month I had to go in there to inventory with Henry and he closed the door behind us. 'Not to lose that cold, Mr. Farrington,' he said and I wanted to say to hell with the cold, leave the door open because what would you do if you couldn't open it? No one could hear you in there with those sides of beef and lamb and pork hanging on hooks, and then Rowling said,"

"'Mr. Farrington.'"

"'He was pointing behind me and I turned to look."

"On the bulkhead, there by the clock, the wind-speed indicator was moving and it hadn't moved since we got underweigh, a square, black box the size of an electric clock with one hand."

"The hand was moving, one white hand on a black face coming up from zero, the beginning of a circle that ended with a hundred. Then the hand took a jump and the wind came on the bridge."

"Rowling went for the port hatch to close

it and when I looked out I couldn't see the sky. The wall was too high and coming too fast and there wasn't any sky left. He leaned in on the hatch and shut it, the rubber gasket into the steel ridge, turned the four dogs and crossed to starboard to close the other hatch."

"Now it was dark and the noise started. Rowling cupped his hands around his mouth and said something but I couldn't hear him. The noise was winding up higher and higher and Rowling was pointing again, at the bulkhead with the clock and the wind-speed indicator. I looked at it. The hands said a quarter after three, one on top of the other straight out to the right, steady at a quarter after three and Rowling was on the sound-powered phone, yelling into it."

"I looked at the wind-speed indicator again and it wasn't a quarter after three. I hadn't been looking at the clock."

"The wind was blowing steadily at seventy-five knots."

<u>III</u>

He stopped speaking, came back to where I was and sat down in the sand. He began to draw again and I tried to see what he had drawn, but all I could see in the moonlight were boxes in the sand.

"Have you ever seen wind like that?" he said.

"No, nothing like that."

He started another box, one line, two, the third twice as long as the first. It wasn't going to be a box.

"Do you remember what it was like to be caught in the schoolyard at recess, in a corner with the cyclone fence on both sides and the boys in front of you?"

"Yes, I remember things like that."

"You can't run, you can't scream or cry, you can't do anything except wait for it to happen, but even that isn't the same. You're only scared of getting hurt and what it will feel like. But with wind like that on a ship you're waiting for the wind to blow you under the water and the seas to roll over as if you were never there at all."

"I can't imagine it," I said but I could imagine something like it. It was what I hadn't told him when he thought I had told him everything, something irretrievable so that the inside of you drops away, as lost as a thing lost in the sea.

He was looking at what he had drawn and began to speak again,

"The Captain was on the bridge by then and John came up through the hatch in the radio room. Outside, on deck, you couldn't stand up or crawl or hold on. Both of the bridge hatches were dogged down, two inch black rubber gaskets pushed out around the combing by the dogs, and it was still blowing on the bridge."

"But now you could stand up without holding on, just stand with your hands at your sides. The sea was down to nothing, blown flat by that wind and you couldn't see. Not the deck down in front of the bridge, the forecastle, the anchors, the forty-millimeter cannon, you couldn't see anything because of the rain."

"It came flat, straight across the water as if there were high pressure hoses out there pointed at us and looking out of the big port-holes forward was just like looking up into a showerhead. It smashed into the glass and even with the wipers on full there was nothing on the glass but water. And then it started to come in, around the gaskets, dripped from the overhead, ran down the bulkheads and pretty soon it was over the bottoms of your shoes. The ship was barely rolling but the water on the bridge ran from side to side sloshing across the deck."

"The Captain came out of the radio room

and bent over the chart table. He walked a pair of dividers along our course line and made a cross. Then he looked up at the clock and wrote a time under the cross."

"And that's where it started, all of it," he said.

A cross on the ocean I thought. If you drew one on a map, in some way it was on the ocean, too. In an animated movie you could actually see a cross on an ocean. I was going to say, "'X' marks the spot of a treasure, or a grave," but I didn't.

"Yes, that's where it started all right," he said, "and maybe that's where it ended, too. But everything we did, everywhere we went afterwards was attached to that cross as if we were run out on a leash."

"'I'll relieve you now, Francis,' the Captain said close to me, almost in my ear."

"'Course 281, speed five knots,' I said in what sounded like a whisper

but was nearly a yell and the Captain

slowed the ship down until we only had steerage way on."

"'We'll...stay...here, ...until we can see,' he said and we almost had to read his lips."

"We waited and you wanted to put your hands over your ears, do anything to stop the screech of that wind like the skidding of cars that didn't crash. And under the howl of the wind the rain boomed against the bridge. You would have sworn it was alive out there, that it was trying to burst through the hatches, blow out the portholes, and wash us into the sea."

"We waited. We watched the wind-speed indicator and then the sea began to rise again. A little at first, the bow up as if there was more water under the ship, and then down the wave with the wind-speed indicator still steady at seventy-five knots. The radar screen was just a blur and there was nothing on the radios but static, and then everyone was holding on."

"A big wave had come, the first one, and we went up on top of it, slipped sideways down the back, and dug our bow into the next one. And I tell you it was like running into a mountain. The ship stopped dead and shook. She shook from one end of her to the other and when the water we took over the bow hit the bridge all the portholes turned white and then they turned green like you were looking into an aquarium."

"'Get that helmsman,' the Captain yelled and Rowling started for the PA but the Captain waved him into the radio room, to go down through the hatch inside and bring the helmsman back himself. And then we started up the side of another one, started to slide back, and the Captain called out loud enough for anyone to hear,"

"'All ahead full!'"

"With both hands on the handles I rang them down and then all the way up and through the deck you could feel the ship stiffen with the two big propellers spinning and the engines wide open."

"Now I had my head down and both arms around the annunciator. I could feel the cool, shiny brass on my face and looking sideways I could see John. In the corner of the bridge forward he was jammed in like a monkey. His face was white, whiter than I had ever seen it, and he was looking at me."

"I looked down, into the polished brass under my face and I could still see. It was a curved picture of everything on the bridge and he was there, in that corner, holding on and staring at me."

"Why?" I said.

He was still drawing in the sand, with a stick now, something he found in the sand beside us, but he didn't answer. I lit a cigarette, handed it to him and lit one for myself. We smoked silently sitting in the sand.

"Why was he staring at you?" I said.

But he didn't answer. He only drew something else with his stick and went on.

"Rowling and the helmsman Stone came up through the hatch and back onto the bridge and Stone tried to take the wheel. The other helmsman wouldn't let go. He wasn't doing anything, steering the ship, easing her into the seas. He was just holding on to the wheel as if it was his job to see that it didn't move. It took both them, Rowling and Stone, to get him away from the wheel and then he just stood there. He was shaking his head back and forth, shaking his head and standing there."

"I tell you it was mad with me wrapped around the engine order telegraph, the Captain holding himself in the door to the radio room, Rowling and Stone, the two of them at the wheel trying to get the ship up into the wind, and John in his corner as if he was hanging there. You would have thought you were in a madhouse."

"The sea was climbing all the time but the rain was slowing. You could see something out there, huge, gray moving things with humped backs and on top of them, more waves long and white and blown by the wind in the air.

"From the top of one of them you could see more around us, the biggest coming from the south-east and the others from everywhere. And some of them were beginning to break white on their tops."

"When we'd finished the drop down the back of one, another would come in over the bow and cover us, bury the bow in ten feet of water with only the black barrel of the forty-millimeter sticking out. They came over the bow and down the deck, with water over your head, smashed into the deckhouse and then ran like rivers along the sides over the combings, and back into the sea."

"'The wind will drop," the Captain said but not to anybody and he didn't look much like a Captain the way he was holding himself in the radio room door with his arms and legs. I swear it looked more like a zoo than the bridge of a ship the way everyone was holding on but we all watched the wind-speed indicator and it did begin to drop, to sixty, then fifty, finally down to thirty knots. And it stayed there."

"I don't know if you know what that means but the wind was at thirty knots through all the rest of it with the seas piling higher all the time, higher and sharper and closer together."

I didn't know what it meant and I didn't ask, but I was always pretty good at doing sums in my head and it didn't seem like very much wind to me.

Thirty knots wasn't even thirty-five miles an hour and you could drive that speed almost anywhere. You could see a sign for

'35 m.p.h.' in every town you were ever in.

"Finally the rain stopped, fell away, blown away, and we could see. There was some light, gray with mist or water in it but enough to see there were no small boats around us anywhere. There was nothing but ocean heaped and broken and running at us from the south-east."

"'Come left to 130,' the Captain said and Stone swung the wheel."

"'Coming left to 130,' Stone said."

"'We've gone beyond them,' the Captain said. 'We have to go back.'"

"'Steady on 130,' Stone said, and we started back where we had come from."

"We ran on that course for half and hour and one by one we found them. With three men on the flying-bridge with binoculars and everyone down on the bridge looking, we found them. They were hove to in the seas, floating up to the tops and down into the troughs like driftwood and there was nothing much left topside on any of them. No dinghies, no life-saving rings, rubber boats, anchors, lines, nothing at all. They were swept clean."

"There would be a man down in the cockpit, or maybe two, hunched down in oilskins and not seeing us, not even seeing us, just trying to keep from being broached. I was counting, John was counting, Rowling was counting and the Captain, too, one boat after another with men in them who must have wished to God they had never come, wished they were home sitting in a chair or lying in a bed, anywhere but where the were."

"'Twenty-three,' I said, and John and then Rowling said,"

"'Twenty-three.'"

"'We're missing one, Captain,' I said but he was back at the chart table writing something on the chart."

"'Helmsman,' he said, 'start a circle north,

outside the furthest boat you can see.'"

"The sea was behind us now and lifting the ship like the palm of a hand, up and up and then it passed under us and we settled, down into the trough where there was no horizon, only the tops of the seas above us in the sky."

"But when the wave motion was right, or wrong, when one of those mountains caught us we went down the front of it like an avalanche, slewing, fish-tailing, nearly out of control."

"But we found it, the twenty-fourth boat. Off to the north, past the last boat we saw it – foundered. They were barely afloat with just the cabin-top out

of water and two men in orange life-jackets were sitting on top of it cross-legged. They rose up with the sea and waved, and down and disappeared."

"The Captain was behind me and he said,'

"'Tell them to stay where they are, Francis.'"

"Everybody knew we had to tell then something. It wasn't going to work just to let them try to swim in those seas because nobody was going to be able to do that. I went outside and the wind blew me right up against the railing. It was as if you had to do everything in slow motion with weights on your arms and legs and I tried to speak to the men on the cabin-top through the loud-hailer,"

"STAY WHERE YOUR ARE...SIT STILL AND DON'T MOVE' and my voice bellowed out again from the speaker but it sounded like something coming out of a hole, or a cave. They couldn't hear me. When they came up the next time one of them had his hand cupped to his ear, but across fifty yards of water you couldn't hear anything in that wind and seas."

"Down on the fore-castle the Bosun and the deck crew were working on the inflatable raft. They had a long line tied to it with floats every three yards and they were trying to get it over the rail but they couldn't stand up down there. They were working on their knees and the Bosun was flat on his stomach so he could use both hands."

"They had to take the life-lines down first, they ran all the way around the ship, and some of the stanchions because there was no way they could lift that raft over the life-lines in the wind. It was like working on the back of a bucking horse, opening turn-buckles, unthreading cable, but they did it. When they had the stanchions down and the life-line secured the Bosun looked up at the Captain."

"'Steer west,' the Captain said and Stone put on left rudder. We ran cross-wind, away from the men on the cabin top, and as we got further away they were waving at us with both arms and one of them was trying to stand up. Both bridge hatches were open now and the wind was coming through like a tunnel. We rolled cross-wind, thirty degrees, thirty-five degrees of roll, and standing out there on the bridge-wing was worse than anything that had happened before, even worse than when the wind had come."

"I was outboard in the corner of the bridge-wing where the railings met and when the ship rolled to starboard I was out over the sea and the only way to look was down. The ship rolled and the sea came up at me gray with waves, then green, and finally white with foam and froth and I could have touched it. I'm sure I could have if I reached down and I was standing ten feet above the deck, twenty feet above the water."

"Then the Captain was out on the bridge-wing,"

"'Bring her around east,' he said, 'and

slowly. Don't take a sea on the bow,' and Stone began the turn. We went around a little at a time with the bow climbing higher and higher as we turned into the seas, and then we were around, running east and the Captain signaled to the Bo-sun."

"Somehow they got the inflatable over the side with all of them lying flat on their stomachs holding onto the side of the raft. It floated down the side and then astern of us moving fast down-wind with its high sides in the wind."

"'Slow ahead,' the Captain said."

"Behind us the raft sailed away down-wind, the line and the floats paying out as we ran cross-wind again back toward the men on the cabin top. The long loop of line floated behind and then we were past them and slowed, and stopped. They were safe, or almost safe with the line floating down to them the raft on one end and us on the other."

"The two of them started to pull hand over hand and the raft came up bouncing and tossing until it was beside them, and then they were in it attached to us by three-quarters of an inch of nylon."

"Stopped the way we were the ship was rolling past the gunwales and with ten feet of freeboard amidships the way she was rolling now there were twenty feet to climb or none at all when the gunwale went under. Wet steel sides to scramble up, be pulled over, wait for the right moment and throw yourself over, but they did it and fell on the deck along with the deck crew lying like clubbed fish."

"'Get them below, Francis,' the Captain said, 'bundle them up.' and I started for the deck, down the ladder from the bridge-wing."

"It was a mistake. We rolled then, to my side, further and further, and I held onto the rail with both my hands harder than I had ever held anything. Finally I knelt with my knees on the steel steps as the sea came up towards me. I knelt and tried to be small, tried to attach myself somehow and felt my hands begin to slip on the wet, white paint and the roll stopped, and we started back up."

"I was shaking when I got to the deck and my hands were in fists with nothing in them. I had almost gone over. Just going down a ladder I had almost gone into the sea. And I tell you it was a sea no man could swim in. It was a sea I had never seen before."

What would it be like to go overboard in seas like that, I thought. You would go over and under the water, then up trying to breathe and looking for the ship, seeing it moving away from you, further and further. You might try to swim, a few strokes, and then just float away back in the wake, a speck in the water and then nothing until you were alone. It would be hard to be more alone than that, very hard.

He had finished his drawing in the sand. It looked like a maze but a simple one, like one you would find in a children's' book.

"The Bosun and three of the crew brought the men into the wardroom and there were seven of us in there, six in life-jackets, six wet men, and one we had brought aboard had no shoes, I got them lying down on the wardroom benches, wrapped them in blankets, and the mess cook brought coffee. I sat in the chair at the end of the table and tried to find out what had happened but only one of them could talk. The other just lay there with his eyes closed, two hands around the coffee cup on his chest with the coffee slopping over when we rolled. One man was up on an elbow, trying to sip at his cup, moving his lips but saying nothing."

"But we had done it. We had saved them and they were all right lying on benches wrapped up to their necks in blankets. In that sea with the wind blowing a gale and more we had pulled them out of an ocean and rescued them. After all that time it was a real rescue and I felt good. I sat in that chair at the head of the table and smiled."

"The one on his elbow looked up at me and tried to smile too."

"'Came too fast' he said. 'We were all right...then the boat was full of water. Maybe the bow came off...or the bottom fell out.' He sipped at his coffee and some of it ran down his chin."

"'We didn't have time,' he said. 'Water came in and there was no boat.... We held the rails and prayed ...couldn't see you or anybody...couldn't see anything ...thought you'd never find us....'"

"He put his coffee cup on the table, laid back on the bench and closed his eyes."

"I got up and went over to the other man and took the cup from his hands and they fell, one on his chest, the other over the side of the bench until it hung with his fingers touching the deck."

"'Are you all right?' I said and lifted his arm, laid it across his chest. He didn't move and then he opened his eyes."

"He looked at me as if he didn't know that he had been saved, that there had been a rescue, and then he said,

"'Did you find...Franklin?'"

"I nodded and said,"

"'He's fine. You've had a bad time but you're safe now. In a few hours you'll be home."

"He shook his head. It looked like it took what was left of him to do it, closed his eyes, and then he said, again,"

"'Franklin?....'"

"I thought he was in shock or maybe delirious."

"He's right over there,' I said and pointed to the other man but he shook his head again."

"' Isn't that Franklin?' I said."

"'Not Franklin.'"

"'You mean there was another man?'"

"He nodded, tried to nod and couldn't."

"'What happened to him?' I said. 'Tell me what happened to him,' but now his head was on one side. His mouth was open and I started for the bridge but before I got to the top of the ladder I looked back at the two men."

"The one who had told me tried to raise his arm and couldn't. It fell and hung down again with his fingers touching the deck and the blankets had moved. Somehow he had pulled them trying to get up or trying to do something and at the end of the bench his feet were uncovered, two white feet with their toes curled from the cold and somewhere out there in the ocean there was another man."

IV

He got up from the sand and stood and looked up at the sky. He seemed gigantic standing there and I was in his shadow, the shadow from the moon. I watched him and then I said,

"There was another man."

"Yes," he said.

"Could he have lived...through that?"

"He could, they do if they want to."

"But he could never have been found."

"He could be found, too, if someone wanted to find him."

"And someone did?" I said.

""Yes," he said, "someone did."

The moon had started down. In an hour it would be gone and already on the other side of the world the sun was climbing. It would be dawn with the red rim of the sun

over the edge of the earth. It would be another day.

He was still standing looking up at the
sky with his back to me, but I could hear
him. I could hear every word.

"On the bridge the Captain had a mug of
coffee in his hand and John was out on the
bridge-wing looking astern where we had
taken them out of the sea. We were back
on 281 and on the way home rolling and
pitching as bad as ever."

""Are they all right?' the Captain said."

"'They're all right,' I said, 'but....'"

"'But what?' he said and it seemed as if
everyone stopped talking but no one was
talking."

"'There was another man.'"

"'A third man in the boat?"

"'Yes, I don't know...he didn't say much,
only, "Where is Franklin?" I thought he
meant the other man, but he didn't.... He
meant someone else.'"

"'There were three men,'" the Captain said.

"'Yes.'"

"The Captain turned and set his mug in the holder by the chart table. He looked down at the chart then up at the clock on the bulkhead, and he said something I couldn't hear."

"'Did you say something, Captain?' I said."

"He took his hand out of his pocket then and rested it on the chart table and we stood there in the gray light with Rowling leaning against the bulkhead and Stone at the wheel. John was still on the bridge-wing but now he stood in the hatchway. He looked at me and then he watched the Captain."

"'You are sure there were three men,'" he said again.

"'Yes, sir.'"

"'Left ten degrees rudder, steer course

112.'"

"'Coming left to 112,' Stone said.'"

"The ship started around and up into the wind, climbing the face of a wave and rolling the gunwale under in the turn. And then we were around again and going back the way we had come, south of the way we had come so we could go back to where we had been. The place somewhere astern John had been looking toward."

"And then he came in through the hatch and over to me and whispered in my ear,"

"'What the Captain said when you told him…?'"

"'A curse?' I said."

"'Or a prayer,' and he went back to looking out at the sea, only now he was looking ahead of us into the waves."

"'Francis,' the Captain said but he didn't sound the same. There was something really wrong now as if a part had broken, a bent shaft, something out of alignment. You couldn't hear it, not yet you couldn't, but it had started somewhere and it wasn't going to stop."

"'I want you to go below and find out,' the Captain said. 'I want the man's name, the condition he was in, whether he had a life-jacket on, and Francis....'"

"'Yes, sir.'"

"'I want to know when he went over. We have to know when he went into the sea.'"

"I started below, again, and it took time. I had to get down through the ship, through the hatch in the radio room, down a ladder built for a monkey, along a cat-walk, through a passageway and then down another ladder into the wardroom. And then I had to get one of them conscious enough to talk, clean up the vomit, the benches, the deck, and I had to stop the one I was talking to from shaking."

"'It came too fast,' he said. 'We were going to rig life-lines, tie everybody together, get the flashlight, but it came too fast.'"

"I didn't hurry him, I wanted to, but I didn't. I wrote everything down, things I didn't need to write down and I wanted to ask the other man the same questions but all he could do was shake his head from one side to the other and then he was sick again."

"It was bad down in the wardroom with the ship rolling the way she was, big, heavy rolls you were sure would never stop, and whenever she would start over the man who was sick would moan. He moaned all the way through the roll until it stopped and we came back up, and then all the way through the next one."

"'When did he go over?' I said and the man I was talking to just nodded."

"'I have to know when he went into the sea,' and I knew why we had to know that, too, because if we were going to look for him he wasn't going to be where he had gone overboard. He was going to be a long way from there by now, somewhere to the north in the Gulf Stream on his way to Labrador."

"'Somewhere near the beginning,' the man said. 'Sometime right after the wind hit us. The water came in and we climbed on the cabin-top and Franklin was gone. I heard him yell once and I think I saw him, I saw something that could have been him. Then he was gone. There was nothing we could do. We couldn't have saved him in anything like that, nobody could.'"

"I got him settled down again and someone to watch both of them and started for the bridge. And I can tell you I was glad to get out of there, the smell was bad, wet clothes and blankets, vomit, sweat, and fear. It has a smell, you know, too."

You hear that fear has a smell, that animals can smell it, and you hear correctly but I said,

"It does?" knowing that it did, never having told anyone, one of the beads I had on my string I had not told him the color of. But I had not felt it when I met him in the road, in the dark. No one could have smelled it then.

He sat back down in the sand, his knees up, drawing in the sand again, the same boxes.

"I was glad to get out of there," he said. "It was embarrassing to be around and with the way the roll was I thought I might be sick. That would have been something, the Executive Officer of a search and rescue vessel sick in the wardroom along with the two survivors, but I didn't get sick."

"I was just plain tired, tired of holding on with both hands every step you took, holding on to wet steel pipes, wet brass rails, holding on down every passageway and up every ladder, and I was tired of running errands. It was what John should have done.

It didn't take me to go down to the ward-room and ask questions with him up there on the bridge where at least you could breathe, where there was air that wasn't full of sweat and diesel oil and the smell of a roast pork with black-eyed peas that no-body had a chance to eat and nobody would ever eat now."

"But I wasn't sent down there to ask questions. I didn't see that until a long time later, but that wasn't why I was down there."

"What do you mean?" I said.

"The Captain didn't send me for that."

"But that was what you said."

"He sent me so I could get myself ready. So I would have time to think about it, about what was going to happen if we ever found him, and I thought about it, too, like thinking about a bad dream. And it was, just like thinking about a bad dream you hadn't even had yet because there wasn't a chance in a million we would ever find him, not in all that water and those kinds of seas."

"'His name is Patrick James Franklin,' I said to the Captain, 'age sixty-four, real estate agent, married, two children, five feet nine inches tall, weight one hundred and seventy-five pounds. He had a lifejacket on, a white canvas one with the cork sewn in, and he was all right when the storm hit. He went over right at the beginning and they never saw him again.'"

"'What time did he go overboard?'"

"'They don't know, at the beginning when the storm hit.'"

"The Captain had the rough log out on the chart table and pencil and paper and he looked up at the Loran receiver on the bulkhead."

"'If that worked there would be a better chance,' he said."

"'If he has any chance at all,' I said and

everything seemed to skip a beat, the chronometer, the ticking of the gyro-compass, the swing of the inclinometer, even the diesels down below seemed to miss a revolution."

"'He has a chance,' the Captain said 'better than some…. We know he's there.'"

"And from the corner by the starboard hatch John said the same thing,"

"'We know he's there,' and he was watching me again, the way he had before like some kind of white bird on a wire or up in a tree."

"We ran back along our track with the Captain watching his stop watch and when we came to the mark he had made on the chart, and remember

it was only a cross on a piece of paper that might be where we were, might be where the man went over, or might be neither of them, he said,"

"'Come left to 000' and he clicked the

watch to stop and then again to start, and we went north, with the sea behind us and the Gulf Stream underneath."

PART THREE

I

He stopped and laid back on the sand, looked up at the stars. The white moon had set and there were millions. I could see them, too, like someone had pricked holes in the black dome of the sky. The Big Dipper was there and the Milky Way and I said,

"Francis?"

"Yes."

\"Would you tell me something?"

"Of course."

"It's a very stupid question."

"Don't be too sure of that," he said.

And he was right because I was sure there

were plenty of people who didn't know the answer, who if you asked them would answer quickly and then stop and be embarrassed. If you made a list of those kinds of things that people thought they knew and didn't, it would be a long one.

"How do you know where you are?" I said.

"What did you say?"

"How do you know where you are on the sea? I mean in the daytime when you can't see the sun or the land."

"You don't," he said.

"You don't know where you are?"

"You make a guess."

"A guess?"

"An educated guess. You call it a 'DR.'"

"And what's . . .?"

"Dead Reckoning," he said.

I had heard that before. It was the way people went places when they didn't know how to go. "I got there by 'dead reckoning', they said but I didn't know what they meant and most of them didn't either.

"It's simple," he said, "you know where you started from, the compass tells you what direction you're going, you know how fast and you know how long. That tells you where you are."

"Does it?"

"No, it doesn't ," he said.

"What does it do, then?"

"It gives you a 'Dead Reckoning Position' that's only a guess because right from the beginning the wind and the currents are pushing you somewhere, somewhere else, somewhere you don't want to be."

He was getting angry but not at me, not at the question I had asked him.

"And you want to know why it's called, 'Dead Reckoning,' don't you?"

"Yes."

"Don't you want to know why I know you want to know that?"

"I do."

"Because you're not the first person to ever ask me," he said.

And she was back again, from wherever she had been, she was back. In some odd way she might have been waiting, not his way but some way, and later, of course, I wondered if she had ever gone.

" And I don't know why it's called that," he said, " I never knew, maybe somebody knows, maybe nobody knows, but I don't."

"It's the way the dead reckon, I guess," he said and sat up. Then he stood up.

"But nobody on that ship thought about where we were for the next hour or two or three, whatever it was, I can tell you that," he said.

"In that time I learned never to worry about a ship's roll again. I didn't care if we rolled forever if only the yawing would stop. I didn't like rolls, never liked them, but the yaw was terrifying. We came down the front of waves and slipped sideways, swerved, with the stern out to the side sometimes so you could see it from the bridge. You could see the stern pushing its own wave in front of

it and any minute it would come around and we'd broach and roll over, and even though everyone knew we were out there, the whole Seventh Coast Guard District from Havana to Georgia by now, we'd roll over and be gone, all those tons of metal and ropes and engines and men down to the bottom in five hundred fathoms."

"And Stone was having trouble I can tell you, the way he swung the wheel. He was trying to out-think those waves coming at us from the stern, waves he couldn't even see until they picked us up and rushed underneath, and sometimes he almost lost it, sometimes he almost lost us."

"The stern would come around and he'd spin the wheel and say,"

"'Can't hold her, sir,' and the Captain or me or John would ring up full speed or stop on the engines for just long enough to bring her back under control and the Captain would say,"

"'Can't change speed too much…we'll lose him.'"

"And I remember thinking to myself – 'lose him?'"

"My God, P.J. Franklin was already as lost as a man could be, but the Captain didn't think so. He didn't think the man was lost as long as we knew he was there, even if he was floating around alone in an ocean."

"We were running along the man's drift. The Captain had picked a time when he had gone into the water, and the place, and we were running north with the Gulf Stream following a drifting man."

"It was lunacy. It looked fine on the chart but it was crazy. The cross was on a piece of paper not on an ocean, on a piece of paper on a table on the bridge, not out there on the sea. You couldn't see anything except those huge, gray seas and even the time was a guess taken from our log when the storm hit. We were guessing where we were, guessing where to turn and when, guessing at the drift from the wind and the seas. The only thing we weren't guessing about was the Gulf Stream. It went north no matter what, as steady as a river."

"'I want four look-outs, Francis,' the Captain said, 'with binoculars and relieved every half-hour. Use the engineers if you have to.'"

"Rowling and I started in on a watch list. With the men we had we'd be through them in three and a half hours but that would be enough. In three and a half hours it would be dark and nobody would be looking for a man in the sea in the dark."

"When the watches were set, when we

were still coming down the front of waves
fish-tailing in the following seas so the
look-outs up on the flying-bridge had to
twine their legs in the railing to use their
hands, the Captain pushed the button on
his stop-watch, looked at the clock, and
wrote something down on the chart."

"'We'll try here,' he said and I swear he
said it as if it was a place where we'd
stopped to fish, as if there was a better place
further on but we were going to try this
one first."

"He started an expanding square search,
two minutes run east – turn - two minutes
north – turn – four minutes west – turn –
and then south for four minutes. We spi-
raled out from the center like a drunk
trying to walk, as if the Captain had him on
the end of a string — only it was a ship on
the other end of the string."

It didn't seem like a drunk on a string to
me. I could see what he had drawn in the

sand, an expansion of lines that doubled, enclosing the center. God knows I had drawn enough of them myself and not known what else they were, except a labyrinth, and for that you did need a ball of string. We had them in common and they were just as much a puzzle to me when I drew them as what happened on that ship was to him.

"And the Captain didn't watch what we were doing, either. He was bent over the chart table calling off minutes from his stopwatch and writing. The other quartermaster, O'Neill, was on the bridge now and he was filling up a page in the rough log with times and course changes but the rest of us were watching."

"John was out on one bridge-wing and I was on the other, Stone and Rowling were looking straight ahead, and there were four look-outs up on the flying-bridge above us. There were eight pairs of eyes all seeing the same thing, gray, gunmetal waves coming from the south-east, the biggest I had ever seen one after another as if they'd never run out, pitching, rolling, yawing us when we went through those course changes every time the Captain clicked his watch."

"It was a lesson I'll tell you in all the ways a ship can move with ten feet of water coming over the bow or the stern swung out or rolling thirty-five or forty degrees. It was like some kind of a lunatic's ride at an amusement park. In the wind and wet, six of us jammed into some kind of contraption that went up and down while it went sideways and around in circles. We were all in it all right and maybe somewhere out there P.J. Franklin was in it, too, and maybe not."

"There wasn't a chance in a million of finding him, of even being in the right place, and if we were, if all the guesses were right, we would never see him in the breaking tops of those waves. There was white water all over the sea, foam and streaks along the direction of the wind and spindrift everywhere."

"And there was less and less light. Up behind that sky packed from one end to the other with clouds the sun was falling, falling faster as it got later, and damned soon it would be dark. Then there would be no chance at all."

"What's 'spindrift'? Francis," I said.

"What's 'spindrift'…?"

"Yes."

"Jesus Christ," he said, "I just don't believe it."

"Don't believe what?" I said but I knew. It was another coincidence that was not one, that you either believe in or not.

"Nothing, nothing that you…but do you understand what it was like out there in the middle of that and then the Captain called out to me on the bridge-wing and I came

in, wet from spray, cold, and tired and tried
to cross the bridge without holding on and
nearly fell into Stone."

"The Captain looked at me as if he
wanted me to tell him what I thought about
things, but I wasn't going to tell him I
thought the whole business was lunacy. I
wasn't going to tell him that we ought to
be back with the others in case one of them
broke down, that we ought to be doing
anything but what we were and I said,"

"'Planes?' and he nodded."

"'Tell Miami we need them,' he said and I
started for the radio room again.

"Inside it was warm, almost hot from the
transmitters and receivers and Collins was
still in his swivel chair with his eyes closed.
His two fingers were moving back and
forth on the CW key in a blur and he had
his headphones on. He wasn't asleep. He
was trying to raise a ship north of us, any
ship. He'd been trying for an hour but no

one was listening or no one was there."

"The Seventh District came up on the first call and I knew Miami Air Station was listening. The duty pilots were saying, 'Christ, can you believe this shit,' and looking out at Biscayne Bay. The seas would be running there, too, running and breaking in the shallow water, no boats, none anywhere, not even the big drag-line would be working in this weather. And down at the end of the runway the wind-sleeve would be straight out from the pole."

"' Request air search – position thirty-seven miles bearing 292 from Great Issac Light –' I said and I said it again so Miami Air could hear. They weren't holding on with one hand down there, jammed against the bulkhead, with my pants wet and shoes full of water."

"The District came on and repeated,"

"'Air search requested – position thirty-seven miles bearing 292 from Great Issac

Light – single man in water – white life-
jacket.'"

"I laughed when I heard that. Nobody
heard me but I laughed when I heard, 'single man in water' because it was the kind of
thing you'd hear in a lunatic asylum. Someplace where every minute or so the floor
tipped and you slid across the room and I
wondered if a single man felt differently
from a married one if he was alone in the
ocean."

"I started for the bridge and looked back
at Collins. He still had his eyes closed, earphones on, his fingers moving and then
stopping to listen. He was working the big
CW transmitter on 500 K, a thousand
miles in all directions trying to find someone else to look for a single man in the
water."

"'They're coming, Captain,' I said but he
didn't hear me. I don't think he knew John
and I were beside him because he was com-

puting drift, the same thing he had been doing for hours. Now he was figuring how far P. J. Franklin had drifted while we were looking for him in the wrong place. And he couldn't make a mistake. Just one along with all the guesses and it was over."

"We ran north some more and were on another search pattern when the first plane came. It was an Albatross, a two-engine seaplane that looked like a duck, a hanging belly under it and two pontoons under the wings like something you'd find in a bathtub. It came from the south flying low and when it saw us it began to circle. The Captain went to the radio and talked to the pilot and the plane climbed and flew off on the first leg of another expanding square."

"Now there were twelve pairs of eyes looking at the sea, eight down below and four up there, and they had even less of a chance of finding the man than we did. Everything was the same down under them, the sea in every direction, white and gray and the same everywhere. They weren't going to find anything in all that water, not the head of a man in a water-logged life-preserver anyway."

"And now it was really getting darker, not dark from the clouds and the storm, but the dark of night coming."

"The plane finished one pattern and started another and there was a buzz on the sound-powered phone from the flying-bridge. One of the lookouts was talking to O'Neill on the head phones,"

"'Helicopter approaching,' he said."

"Then we could hear it, the same sound they always made, as if they were broken , the blades going around and around and only just keeping them in the air. It was the right sound for that operation, too, a crazy sound to go with the seaplane flying back and forth above us and the ship rolling and pitching down below and I thought of the old man at the carnival who turns the handle on the calliope. You know who I mean?"

"Yes."

"And I'll tell you something."

"What is it?" and I stood up. I walked over next to him.

"I knew who was turning that handle."

"The man in the sea," I said, "P.J. Franklin?"

"No," he said, "not him," and he laughed a demented laugh so much like a crow or a goat it could have frightened you.

"It wasn't him," he said, "it wouldn't have been him. — He wasn't...what did they call him? ...a single man," and he laughed once more, walked back down to the water's edge, and began to speak again.

"The helicopter started out to starboard close to the sea and even the bright orange paint on it faded in the light. It was having trouble in the wind. Broadside to the wind it was being pushed around and up, and sometimes down."

"Finally the seaplane gave up, not enough light he radioed, and he dipped his wings and headed south. I watched him go from the bridge-wing, just a wing, a point, and then nothing, not even a sound."

"We were on our fourth or fifth search pattern now rolling and pitching in those seas that would never stop it seemed until the end of the world. And then the light in the sky went out, no twilight, just out like a knob had been turned all the way down."

"Up on the flying-bridge the searchlight switched on and you almost had to laugh at that, too. It was thin, a pathetic pencil of light that might have reached fifty or seventy-five yards and then in the sky off to starboard everything was as bright as the inside of a gymnasium. There was white light in the sky, blinding white light like a flash-bulb that stayed on and shone down into the sea."

"It was the high-intensity lamp the helicopter carried under its belly.

You could find something with that if you had the patience and were in the right place. It showed up a circle of sea the size of a parking lot, white light you couldn't look at, that left red spots in your eyes if you did. And you couldn't see the helicopter anymore. You could only hear it and see the circle of light traveling around under it."

"But the helicopter wasn't flying level. Sometimes it would lean away with the light and nearly shine it up into the sky and once it leaned and shone that thing straight at us. It lighted the ship from end to end, the white paint shining in the wet as if we had just painted her, caught us for a moment at the top of a wave like a flash photograph in black and white."

"They don't like it in the wind and the

dark flying down close to the sea. If they make a mistake it just reaches up and pulls them down into the waves like a bee in a bucket. And then the big light went out and with the rotor roaring in the background the pilot's voice crackled over the loudspeaker on the bridge,"

"'Coast Guard Aircraft YU-14 to Coast Guard Cutter Travis,' and you could hear Collins on the transceiver,

"Go ahead YU-14.'"

"There was a roar on the speaker and it crashed out on the bridge,"

"'…conditions preclude further search… returning to base…repeat…returning to base…acknowledge,' and Collins stuck his head out of the radio room,"

"'Captain, what…?'"

"'All right!' the Captain said and I can tell you everyone could hear him. He wasn't happy. There were plenty of things he wasn't happy about and the helicopter and its light was one of them."

"'Tell him to go home,' he said and you could almost hear him say, 'and tell him to stay there.' He didn't like to hear anybody say they were going home, ever, and now everybody had, except us. We were still there and now it was night."

I remembered that happened back in the schoolyard he had talked about, too, the one with the cyclone fence. Three or four standing around with the sun going down and pretty soon the cars would have lights on. You could hear people calling, somebody's mother or sister, and one by one they would walk out the gate and away down the street in the blue evening until there was no one left except you.

"And that wasn't the end of it?" I said.

"No, it wasn't."

"But in the dark, on the ocean...one man?"

He stood there looking at that ocean and

said nothing. Then he said,

"No, that wasn't the end of it. It's hard to believe, even for me now, but that was only a beginning."

"It was as if there were just the two of us out there, the ship and the man in the sea — P.J. Franklin. And I can tell you, someone could start thinking some pretty strange things after all that had happened already, and all that was still waiting."

"Like what?" I said and I wondered if those things were something I wanted to hear. There are some things people can tell you it is better not hearing at all.

"It was as if there were two of us out there," he said it again, "and you didn't know who was looking for whom."

"What in the world does that mean?"

"As if P.J. Franklin was looking for <u>us</u>," he said.

"Well," I said, "he was, if he was alive he was."

He looked at me.

"You don't know what I mean, do you?"

"No, I don't," I said and wished I hadn't. Maybe I wasn't the first to say I didn't understand it.

He didn't speak for a long time and then he walked back up the beach and sat down where we had sat before. I followed him, trying to think of a way to say I understood something that I didn't.

"Well," he said, "I was sure it was over then but just the same we'd begun another leg of a another pattern miles from where we started if it was the right place to start, if we'd come the right distance, if there was a man there at all. We were running west with our searchlight out, poking around in the dark like a blind man's stick"

"We'd used everything we had, ships, planes, helicopters and you'd think there wasn't anything else to use, but there was. There was still something else, something I didn't know enough about to know we had."

"What was that?" I said.

"You couldn't turn it on with a knob or call it up on the phone or take it out of a locker because then the Captain said the way he'd said it before,"

"'All right!'"

"We all turned and looked at him. He was a soft-spoken man and what he said wasn't loud but it was loud enough to hear the edge of both of those words. He was leaning with his back to the chart table, his two hands on the

edge, and then in the light from the binnacle, the gyro-compass, the green dials

of the radar, he raised up that hand with the two stiff fingers and pointed it at us."

"'Relieve the lookouts,' he said. 'Set a new watch-list. And tell them and whoever's on that searchlight I want every square foot of the forward quadrants covered. And get

Malloy up here.'"

"'And one more thing,' he said and while he said it he looked at every single one of us one after another — 'we're going to find this man. Don't think for a moment that we won't…. And remember this, all of you…' and there wasn't a sound on the bridge except the sound of the sea,"

"'If you don't think we can find P.J. Franklin, then you don't belong out here.'"

"We were stunned, we all were. Nobody had ever heard the Captain say anything like that before or heard him say it the way he did. It was as if there had always been two of him, one behind the other, the one you saw every day and the other one who stepped out of a shadow when you had to find a man in the sea."

"All the time I was looking at his hand, the one with the two stiff fingers. He was holding a pair of dividers in it that were an inch or two apart. I was fascinated by those

dividers because the distance they were
measuring could save P.J. Franklin or lose
him. And that was what we had left after we
had used everything else — two stiff fingers
and a pair of dividers."

"We moved then, O'Neill to get Malloy,
Rowling to change the look-outs, John back
out on the bridge-wing and before he
stepped over the combing he smiled back at
us. In the milky blue light of the searchlight
he smiled first at the Captain, then at me,
and he was gone in the dark."

"But right then, when he looked back, I
knew what that smile meant.

He wanted it like this. He wanted all of us
out there where if you let go at the wrong
time it was a broken leg or a concussion.
And if it was the wrong time and the
wrong place it would be over the cat-walk
and down into the engine room or over the
side and into the sea."

"I would have sworn to it right there on

the spot, and I was right. It was the only thing I was right about and it took a long time to find out that I was. Because I'm telling you John had made up his mind hours ago, when he was looking down at that chart and seeing something I didn't know was there."

He was up again, he'd been up and down half a dozen times in the last hour pacing around, going down on his haunches to poke in the sand, standing with his hands on his hips looking at the sea. There was some light now, enough to know the sun would come. The sand around us was marked with his pacing, tracks going this way and that but always coming back.

I had made a place for myself in the sand. It was hard but better than trying to follow him around. He would walk off five or ten yards and I couldn't see him but I could hear him. His voice came through the end of that night as if he was sitting right next to me. It carried, that voice did, and then he'd come and stand with his back to me, looking up or out. Finally, I said,

"He was the one?"

"Yes," he said, "he was the one, as fresh out of the Academy as if he had been delivered in a box."

"And the smile...?"

"Because that was how he wanted it...like a plan...the tornado, the storm, the lost man, just as if it was all...."

"His plan," I said.

"Yes."

"He was the enemy you didn't know you had?"

"Yes," he said, "he was one of them."

II

I wondered if everyone had an enemy they didn't know they had. It would be like an assassin waiting, following you around and waiting for some time when the time was right. And suppose there was more than one? It was not something to think about and he didn't want to, either.

"That feeling was so strong as if John was just biding his time you could tie a knot in it and I went over to the other bridge-wing. I wanted to be as far away from him as I could get and then Malloy was on the bridge."

"'Flares, Malloy,' the Captain said. 'How many do we have?'"

"'The illumination flares, sir?'"

"'Yes.'"

"'Twelve, sir'"

"'One every ten minutes, Malloy, until they're gone.'"

"'Yes, sir,' he said and then he did that smart about-face we always laughed at."

"The big magnesium flare went up into the black with a 'CRUMP,' burst above us, and started down on its parachute. It could have helped because it lighted up plenty of sea, if it hadn't been for the wind. As soon as it went off up there in the dark it was a blinding point of light like a huge sparkler showing the sea like a porcelain plate, and then the wind took it and blew it away. The flare sailed off downwind closer and closer to the waves and went in like a cigarette in a snow bank."

"Every ten minutes one of them went off as regular as clockwork, 'CRUMP', then nothing while it traveled up in the dark, the burst of white, and it blew off downwind. You couldn't even hear it when it went into the water."

"In two hours we'd used them all and nobody had seen a thing except the waves, one after another like herds of buffalo, and then Malloy was back on the bridge."

"'Illumination flares exhausted, sir,' he said."

"The Captain was looking out the forward porthole now, too, looking along with everybody else. He nodded to Malloy and I thought to myself 'exhausted' wasn't the word for it. We'd been searching in those seas for more than half a day and into the night holding onto something for every minute of it. And it wasn't a hand for yourself and a hand for the ship, either. It was both hands for yourself."

"We weren't going to find anybody in all that water, one old man floating with most of him underwater, probably all of him by now. Even if he had white hair we wouldn't find him and to show you how light-headed I was, I thought of the man sitting in the boat waving a mop at us. A white head of hair shrunken down like a trophy. And when this was all over, I thought, we wouldn't even have that to show for it."

"The Captain was running north again to start another expanding square. On the chart, in that gray cobweb of pencil lines, we were moving north all the time. We'd pass Jacksonville, Charleston, Norfolk, New York, Boston and then swing east with the North Atlantic Drift, across an ocean, down in the Azores Current, and into the Sargasso Sea. A MARIE CELESTE with all of us bones, searching in the weed for a skeleton in a life-jacket."

"I don't know how much later, on one leg or another of a search pattern, the buzzer from the flying-bridge went off. Everyone just looked at it, a metal box on the bulkhead painted white with a wire running into it, and then it went off again."

"Rowling and I went for it at the same time and tried to tear the earphones out of each other's hands. I got the head-set on with one earphone on and one off and the microphone hanging down,"

"'Bridge!' I said and it sounded like I was

talking in a tomb. No one had said a thing for hours and the only thing you could hear was the course changes – 000 – 090 – 180 – 270 over and over again like some kind of chant."

"'Bridge!' I said it again."

"'I think I saw something, sir,' the voice came into my ear."

"'Captain,' I said."

"He came across the bridge, took the head-set, and spoke into the microphone,"

"'Report it right, sailor – bearing and range.'"

"There was nothing coming out of the phone, as if whoever was up there was trying to remember how to say it."

"'Off the port bow, sir, pretty far off,' he said. 'I just saw it when the searchlight went by and then it was gone.' He knew who he was talking to, you could hear it in his voice."

"'Come left, Stone,' the Captain said.

'Make it a slow circle…Francis, tell whoever's on the searchlight to cover the port
quarter forward,' and I went out on the
bridge-wing and up the ladder to the flying-bridge."

"Up on top the wind was blowing hard
out of the dark and the roll and pitch were
worse. A quartermaster was on the searchlight, his legs wide apart, holding onto the
handles with both hands.

"'*Search to port!*'" I yelled in his ear and
he swung the light left and started to move
it across the water. There was light on the
flying bridge, that blue milk light from the
searchlight, and the lookouts kept their
binoculars close to their eyes to keep it out.
There were four of them in a row and with
their black watch-caps pulled down tight
they looked like actors in some eerie play
with their faces made up fish belly white."

"And then one of them yelled,"

"'*Hold it!*'" and the man with the searchlight stopped and held the light steady on a place in the sea."

"'*Back!*' the man said. '*Keep it steady and move it back,*' and the searchlight moved left, slowly, showing one wave top after another with heavy shoulders of sea below them."

"'*There! – right there – don't move it!*' and the searchlight stopped.

"Something was floating in the water. It rose up and then down in a trough, something we had found in the sea."

"'*Don't lose it,*' I said to the man on the light."

"'*No, sir,*' he said and I went for the voice tube down to the bridge. I was still watching whatever it was. The blue beam of light held it like something on the end of an icicle."

"'*Object in the water,*' I said, '*thirty degrees off the port bow, one hundred yards,*' and I felt the ship slow, turn more to port,

and then the engine room bells clanged signaling them down below to throw out the
clutches, the propellers spinning slower and
slower until they stopped."

"The engines idled but the ship was still
moving, she still had weigh on and we
ghosted closer to whatever was there on the
end of the searchlight."

"We had found something. To find anything in that ocean in the dark with those
seas running was a miracle all by itself. But
it didn't look like a sixty-four year old man
— it looked more like a box. A white,
wooden box that had floated off somebody's dock or was thrown over from a
freighter. And now it was drifting along in
the Gulf Stream until somebody in Ireland
or Scotland or the Canary Islands found it
on a beach and burned it for firewood."

"But it wasn't just a box. When it came
up on a wave and turned, floated around in
a half-circle, there was something on the

back of the box."

I sat up. From where I was in my place in the sand, I sat up and clasped my arms around my knees.

"It looked like it had grown there, that the box had been in the sea long enough for something to grow on it, and then it swung all the way around and it was gone."

"'There's a man on it,' somebody said and the engine room bells went off and gave a nudge to the propellers. Then the engines idled again. We were closer and the box swung around and stayed there."

He was sitting in the sand not three feet away from me now and speaking clearly, but I listened like a whisper.

"There was somebody. He had both arms around the box and you could see his head but no face, the back of his head with the face hard up against the box. It went down into a trough below the wave tops, came up, and there was just the box again."

"I thought the next time it came up he would be gone and I remember in a strange way I almost wished he had, then we could start out again to look for him, but he didn't go away. We came closer, thirty or forty yards and you could see it was a man, a man in a white life-jacket holding onto the box. But he didn't look alive."

"He looked like he had locked his hands around that box and put his head down and drifted, drifted for a day and most of a night in those seas seeing nothing but the box against his face, going up and then up some more on the waves, then down wondering about sharks and then not wondering anymore, dead against the box with his hands locked."

"But we couldn't lose him now unless he just dropped off and sank right there in five hundred fathoms. We were close enough so the searchlight stayed on him as if he was on a stage and we waited for him to do something, wave or yell or cry , but he didn't. He didn't do anything."

"We were headed into the wind with the engines turning over enough to keep us there, bucking the seas coming at us, climbing one and then another and straining like a dog on a leash attached to a man in the water."

"We had found him. Against odds longer than a sweepstakes' we had him out there bound to us by something, luck, stubbornness, fate, I don't know what. It was a tie I'd thought could have snapped at any time but I was wrong. It was as heavy and sure as a hawser and right there on the chart to see."

"There was one gray pencil line thin as a thread that connected all those expanded squares, that always moved north leaving the empty squares behind, all empty until the last...."

"And he was in it," I said.

"He was."

"The man who went over, P.J. Franklin?"

"Yes, him."

"It doesn't seem possible," I said and he let out that laugh of his again, a croak or a bark.

"Doesn't seem possible?" he said.

"No, not in those conditions, not the way you've told me."

"You don't believe me then," and he got up. He stood up and looked down at me sitting in the sand and said again,

"You don't believe me."

"I believe you," I said not knowing then if I did or not. "I only said it doesn't seem possible."

"It was possible all right," he said standing there above me. "Later on I thought it was the only possible thing about it. It was the only thing that could have happened."

I didn't know what he meant. But nobody could have guessed what finding P.J.

Franklin would mean and even now, after all this time, what it meant does seem impossible.

I looked up at him and said in a way I hoped would sound like I believed him,

"And then what happened?"

"Do you really want to know?" he said.

"Yes, I do."

"You want to know what happened to P.J. Franklin, don't you?"

"Yes."

"Anybody would want to know that."

"Of course," I said and stood up. I moved closer to him,

"But I want to know what happened to you."

He waited and he shook his head the way a horse will who has run around and around the walls of his corral. Then he went on.

"The ship was pitching even more with the propellers just turning over but now you could hear. The roaring of the engines, the commands, the clanging of the bells were gone and you could hear the sea. Through the hatches, out on the bridge-wing you could hear the seas hissing along the tops and rumbling underneath, smashing over the bow so the ship shook. And they were breaking."

"They broke down the fore-castle in a rush like a river in rapids. It was pitch black night but the searchlight, the lights from the bridge, the all-weather lights in their glass covers showed the white of the waves."

"It was nearly over I thought, what I had been waiting for, even if we didn't know whether P.J. Franklin was alive or dead. Either way, though, it had been like looking for a man who didn't want to be found, like going from house to house, up the steps and in the front door and he would be out the back."

"Plenty of times we must have been going to where he was, where he should be, and when we got there and began to look he would be gone. Or we would be ahead of him and begin to search and he would drift through where we had already been. It was only the line on the chart and the Captain that drew it, and Stone on the wheel following a line he couldn't even see."

"And then down on the bridge the Captain called,"

"'Rowling, get the Bosun and the duty engineer. I want them in the wardroom.'"

"And he called again,"

"'Francis – John, we'll go below.'"

"We went down the ladder and along the passageway, down another ladder with the Captain in front moving fast. As we walked and climbed the speakers inside the ship came on and Rowling's voice filled the ship,"

"'Bosun and duty engineer to the wardroom- on the double!'"

"The Captain sat in his chair at the end of

the wardroom table. The two men we had down there were in bunks in the officer's quarters and I sat inside on the bench next to the Captain where I always sat. John was at the other end of the table and nobody was saying anything. We just sat there holding on and waiting and then the Bosun came in. He stood by the table with his hands down along his sides and his hat in his hand."

"'Get them ready, Bosun,' the Captain said, 'the same crew as before, plenty of line and break out a new . . .,' and the duty engineer came in."

"He stood behind the Bosun with a day's growth of black beard on his face and a white rag in his hand. He was trying to clean his hands with it, working it in between his fingers as if he was going to have to shake somebody's hand."

"'Break out a new life-preserver, Bosun, and bend a line onto it,' the Captain said.

'We'll bring him in and roll him into the inflatable, bring him aboard in the litter.'"

"'Yes, sir,' the Bosun said and he started to say something else but he stopped and looked at us, first at me and then at John, and started for the hatch.

Before he was out of the wardroom he had his hat on and the duty engineer put the hand with the rag in it behind his back."

"'I want an emergency light rigged forward, Wilson,' the Captain said, 'all-weather, fix it to light up the fore-castle and as fast as you can.'"

"'Ten minutes, sir,' he said. He stood there for a moment more and then he said,"

"'I won ten dollars, sir.'"

"The Captain nodded."

"'Get on that light,' he said and the engineer saluted, tried to salute with that rag still in his hand."

"But don't think I thought about the Bosun and his hat and the engineer with his rag, not then I didn't, because everybody in that room was thinking about something else. I saw them all right, smelled the paint and the oil so I've never forgotten how it was in there at three o'clock in the morning with everyone except the engineer soaking wet, cold and wet and tired."

"It is just like some incredible family portrait with the Captain at the end of the table, his hands on top of it one on top of the other and his two stiff fingers sticking out. The table had a green felt cloth flat and green like a billiard table and in the back of my mind I thought there ought to be billiard balls out there, a red and two whites so the three of us could sit there and watch the end of an impossible shot."

Why I said it I will never know but then I said,

"One of the white balls has a spot on it."

"I don't remember that," he said.

"But it does. It has a small red spot."

"Why?"

"So you can tell one of the white balls from the other."

And he began to laugh again only this time he didn't stop. He laughed the way you do at the best joke you've ever heard, long and exhausting until you can hardly breathe and have to stop.

"What is so funny about that? I said.

He got his breath back and said,

"I'll tell you what's so funny, it's a coincidence you will never believe because somewhere on that ship a life-preserver was being taken out of a locker.

Somebody would look it over for a rip or a tear, squeeze it to see if the flotation was there, and then tie a line on it. And if it was tight-laid line with no weak strands, no place where it had rubbed, and tied solid to a canvas strap that might or might not be strong enough to hold the weight of a man in those seas, two men if whoever it was made it out there to P.J. Franklin and back, we could…and then the Captain said,"

"'We'll have to go in and get him and right away. We can't take the ship in and we can't launch a boat.'"

"There wasn't a person on that ship who didn't know it already, who hadn't figured it out as soon as they saw P.J. Franklin on that box. From the mess cook up they knew somebody was going to have to go in after him and they were thinking about the line and the life-jacket, too."

"If it parted, if the stitching came loose or the canvas strap tore, he would drift off downwind in the seas away from the ship, and what would we do then?"

"There would be two men to choose from and only one searchlight and by the time the Captain got one of them, if he got one, the other would be gone. He would be drifting north with the Stream, another man to be looked for, another line on the chart, more expanded squares, with odds so long of the Captain being able to do it twice that not even an engineer would bet."

"'We'll have to go in and get him,' the Captain said but there wasn't any 'we' about it. He wasn't going to go and no one was going to ask him. It had to be somebody else. It had to be a volunteer but who in the name of God would go?"

"Over the side in the dark with seas like that. Who would be crazy enough to do it? Just stand there on the deck of the ship and jump over into that water in the middle of an ocean? Oh no, you would have to be a madman to do that."

"And even if there was somebody he couldn't begin to swim if he wasn't already smashed against the side of the ship just getting into the water. Trying to swim with tons of water coming at you every second, water in the air so you couldn't breathe, thrown upside down, buried under it and <u>still</u> try to swim fifty yards to a man who might already be dead and then trying to swim back? Can you imagine having to swim back with him — dead or alive?"

I couldn't imagine it. It was like something out of a movie you would walk out at the end of shaking your head. You would wonder how they could think such things up and how could they make them look real because things like that didn't really happen. And then I thought, what if they did?

"But I know what you're thinking," he said, "and I thought that, too. What if you did it? What if you came up in those seas and did swim in them, up the sides of hills and down into valleys. If you got there and got him and somehow got back, doing the damned thing twice, two times more than anyone could have asked — if you did that anyone who would ever know you would know you had done it."

"And even people who didn't know about it would know because you would be different from them, someone else for the rest of your life. That's what you're thinking, isn't it?

"Yes," I said, it was what I was thinking. Doing something like that would make you different for the rest of your life the way some few people are different, people you meet and wish you were them.

If you only saw them walking down a street you could tell, or coming into a room, because they had done something you could never do, you would never do, a favour offered and accepted, and carried with them always.

"Like catching the gold ring on a carousel," he said, "that only comes around once?"

"Yes, just like that," I said, "just that way."

"It isn't that way," and he smiled at me,

even in the dark.

"What do you mean?"

"I mean what I said. It isn't that way. It isn't the way you think at all."

We were silent. For some reason he was angry, or disappointed, and the smile meant that he had heard what he had expected, something ordinary from an ordinary man. He turned from me and went on,

"'We'll muster the deck crew forward,' the Captain said, 'put the raft over the side and lash her to the ship. When the man is alongside we'll roll him into it, tie him into the Stokes Litter and bring him on deck.'"

"And as the Captain spoke he was talking to me, not to John and not between us, but to me as if I was the only other person in the room."

"'We'll have the sea on the quarter,' he said, 'there'll be nothing breaking on the fore-castle,' and he said that as if he was offering me something, not very much but all he had."

"But John was the deck officer, it should have been his job to muster the crew but this was no deck drill and the Captain wanted me. Law school, OCS, Executive Officer, second in command, a man he had drunk coffee with for four and half years and tried to convince that the service was his career.

'You'll have your own ship,' he used to say, 'You'll have a command,' because, you know, he thought he knew me. He thought he knew and he looked at me with his hat pushed back on his head, his face wet, both arms on the table and on the end of one of them, a hand with two stiff fingers."

"I said nothing. In that moment when there was a chance to say, 'Yes, sir,' I said nothing. I didn't nod. I dropped my head so I couldn't see the Captain's face and that was answer enough. It answered the ques-

tion that hadn't even been asked but everyone knew had to be, the only one that
made any difference."

"The Captain had been right about everything else, about the cross he had made in
an ocean, about the drift, about when and
where but this time he was wrong and he
turned and looked at John."

"'When you've got them mustered,' he
said, 'call for a volunteer. Get the life-jacket
on him, put the Bosun on the end of the
line and tell whoever it is to go and bring
the man in.'"

"'Yes, sir' John said and got up. He
looked like he was going to say something,
not to the Captain, not to me, maybe to
someplace on the green table between us
but he didn't and the Captain said,

"'You understand that, John, don't
you?'"

"'Yes, Captain,' he said and he was gone.
I was looking at the table. There was no

other place to look."

"'I'll need you on the bridge, Francis,' the Captain said. 'You take the man below when we've got him aboard,' and he stood up and went out through the hatch."

"I watched him go up the ladder, his head, back, legs, feet and I was alone. The only thing that moved in the wardroom was the inclinometer on the bulkhead. It was another clock keeping time from three to nine.

<u>III</u>

"And someone volunteered?" I said.

"Yes."

"He must have been mad."

"In a way he was."

"Someone just said, 'I'll go,' and he walked over to the side and went in?"

"Pretty much like that," he said. "It could have been that way. I wasn't down there to see."

"Why would anyone do it?" I said but I knew there were reasons, reasons enough for some but not for me. If 'the heart has reasons reason doesn't know,' there are other parts of the body with reasons, too.

"I know," he said.

He brushed sand over the boxes he had drawn.

"I know why. It's what I wanted to explain to her but I never had the chance. I never could find her after I knew."

He didn't say why, not then, and when he did the difference it made to me was the difference it might have made to her. If he had found her, if he had ever had the chance to tell her. I thought then and I think now that no matter what you do or how hard you try, it was only once upon a time that people lived happily ever after.

He was standing again with his back to me but not looking at the sea or the sky. He was looking down the beach.

"They were out on the fore-castle when I got back on the bridge, just shadows down there in the edge of the searchlight. They were knee-deep in white water coming at them down the deck and the Captain brought the ship around and put the wind and seas behind us on the quarter."

"Then the light came on, rigged through a forward porthole, the big, all-weather deck light that lit everything like a curtain going up. It was bright out there with colors and shapes and you could see the edges of everything. You could see John with his yellow hair and no hat."

"There were ten of them, eight of the deck crew in dungarees, the Bosun with his blue hat pulled down over his ears and John in his khakis. They were holding coils of line and the Bosun had an orange life-jacket. He was holding it in his hands like a coat."

"The crew were together in a bunch with the coils of line in their hands, then the Bosun, and then John and he was saying something or trying to say something in the wind. It didn't take long whatever it was because he turned his back and held up his arms for the life-jacket. He got it on, turned around, the Bosun pulled on the straps and tightened the buckles, and it was just like he was getting somebody ready to go out and play in the snow."

"Then John stepped over to the side. The Bosun was holding a coil of line and one of the seamen was holding him and John stood there at the edge waiting for the ship to roll to port, and he went over."

"He just stepped over. It wasn't far to go with the sea past the gunwales and he went over and we rolled to starboard. He was gone with only the line going out and the Bosun holding it in both hands and the seaman holding him so he wouldn't go too. Then we rolled back to port again."

"He was out there. You could see the orange in the light from the searchlight. He was gone down into a trough and then up, high up on the side of a wave almost to the top and down, further and further down so we couldn't see him."

"And he wasn't swimming, not any stroke anybody had ever seen, his arms were moving but it wasn't swimming. It was someone trying to stay alive, trying to move something he couldn't move or even see. He wasn't going anywhere, except up and down, way, way up and then down into another trough and we couldn't see him at all."

"The searchlight was still on the white box, a blue line in the dark with the waves climbing up to it and down on the deck the crew were putting over the raft. There were seven of them trying to do it without going over themselves, knee-deep in water when we rolled the gunwale in. They were trying to get it over with one hand and holding on with the other. Then three of them went down on their knees and pushed and it was over bouncing and pounding against the side of the ship like it was trying to get back in."

"The crew moved away from the edge and hung onto the forty-millimeter and the Chief Bosun and the man holding him were the only two out on deck. The Chief was on his knees and the man behind him flat out on his stomach holding onto the Chief's legs. And he was holding the line as if he had a fish on it the end of it, keeping a strain but not enough to pull the hook out and letting the line out a yard at a time."

"I watched it all from the bridge and thought when they pulled the line in hand over hand they'd have something dead on the end of it or nothing at all.

We couldn't see him and maybe he was going down. Maybe he had taken in so much water he was just going down life-jacket and all. He would sink and pull out line behind him until there was no more left, just a weight hanging on the end of a hundred yards of line."

"And that was when I thought about it up there on the bridge looking out through the glass."

"About what?" I said.

He was sitting down beside me again in the sand.

"I couldn't hear you," he said. "Were you asleep?"

"I wasn't asleep."

"It's nearly morning," he said and looked down the beach to the east.

Then he said,

"Why do you listen to this?"

I didn't know what to say. I thought he knew. I thought he understood so I said,

"You listened to me."

"That was yesterday."

"And now it's today," I said. "What difference does it make what day it is? What was it you thought about?"

"You really want to hear that," he said. "It's not very nice."

"Yes, I want to hear it. You've already told me the worst and, yes, I want to hear it."

"No I haven't."

"You haven't what?"

"Told you the worst," he said and was silent. I waited for him to speak and then he did,

"I wanted him to go down. To the bottom. The line to part and him to sink straight down to the bottom with three thousand feet of ocean over him. I wanted the Chief to pull that line in and there to be nothing on the end of it, just another piece of frayed line to throw in a locker."

"I've never thought that about another human being before or after and I watched from the bridge, waiting, but he wasn't going down. The angle of the line was wrong for that. It went out from the side of the ship and he was still there doing something. He was still trying to swim through the seas to the man on the box so he could turn around and swim back."

"For a long time we couldn't see him in the water and then something was there because there was more at the end of the searchlight. There was something more hanging on the box."

"Everyone was watching. Rowling and O'Neill and Collins from the radio room and down below all the hatches were open on the port side and men were jammed in them, the rest of the crew trying to see, dungaree shirts, T-shirts, an engineer with no shirt at all and even the cook, everyone was watching except the Captain and Stone."

"Then there was a sound, it might even have been a cheer, all the way down the side of the ship because the searchlight had moved. It had finally moved away from the box and was holding something else in its beam."

"It was John and the man all right, the two of them so close together they were only one thing, an orange and white bundle thrown up and then buried in the waves. John was trying to swim with only one arm and I watched them come a yard at a time and I looked back at the white box. It was drifting out of the light, into the shadows, into the seas and then it was gone."

"Hand over hand the Chief was bringing in line. There was a strain on it but not enough to haul them through the water. Up on the flying-bridge above me I could hear one of the look-outs,"

"'Why don't they just pull them in?' and another one said,"

"'Drag them under – or part the strap. He'll have to swim.'"

"And he was because they were closer now, almost close enough to see there were two people, one with his arm around the other, kicking, reaching out with his arm, and the other doing nothing. They were coming. Somehow he was moving the two of them through the water and then they were near the raft and one of the seamen jumped down from the deck into it."

"We almost lost him. He didn't have a grip and started to go over. The raft was going ten feet in the air on a starboard roll and smashing down on the water when we rolled back and the seaman just threw himself down in the bottom and lay there."

"John and the man were five yards outboard of the inflatable rising and falling with the seas. When we rolled hard to port you could see them like day in the forecastle light and the searchlight tipped down shining on the two of them in the breaking seas and spray."

"The Captain was behind me on the bridge-wing."

"'Secure the searchlight,'" he said and above us the light went out —blue, white, rose, but just as the light died out I remember the color of the faces on the bridge — rose-colored, the same as they had been just before the storm had come. Before we knew anything about drift and planes and P.J. Franklin, before we had nearly rolled and pitched ourselves to death, before…."

I stood up and held him by the arm. It was not the same as I had held him when I thought he would walk into the sea, but it was nearly the same. And he pulled away.

"John had one hand on the raft and the other was holding the man around his chest. Their heads were side by side and the seaman in the raft reached for them. He was holding himself in with his knees and he grabbed the man and pulled. He tugged at him like he was trying to pull a rug from under a piano but he couldn't do it."

"The man was too heavy or John was holding him. It looked like John wouldn't let him go and then he did and the man rolled into the raft face down."

"The crew lowered the Stokes litter then and got P.J. Franklin into it, pulled and hauled and strapped him into the metal framed stretcher and then all of them lifting on the lines, they brought him up onto the deck."

"'Get the man below,' the Captain said to me, 'I'll be down when John's aboard.'"

"I nodded and turned, started for the hatch down through the radio room. Rowling and O'Neill and Collins were standing behind me on the bridge-wing and I staggered from a roll, fell into Collins, and from behind me I heard,

"'Sorry, sir,' and I kept going through the bridge into the radio room and down through the hatch."

"We got P.J. Franklin below, dragged him through a hatch and down the ladder into the wardroom. We did the best we could in the roll and pitch and laid him out on one of the benches. I got the lifejacket off him. It was an old, white one with pieces of cork sewn into pockets and heavy as lead when I got it off. He was stretched out with blankets around him and I knelt on the deck to see if he was breathing."

"I rubbed his hands and feet, got his mouth open, all the things they taught you, tried to find his pulse and couldn't. I was ready to give him mouth-to –mouth, bring him back to life if I could, if there was a way. I was ready to do anything because it was pretty grim in there with P.J. Franklin."

"And then I put my ear down next to his face and he was breathing but that was all. Just small breaths he'd learned with the waves breaking over his head. His eyes were closed and his face was the color of paper but he was alive."

I sat with him for a long time. I didn't want to go back up on the bridge. There was nothing for me to do up there. I told them P.J. Franklin was breathing, his color coming back a little, and I was staying there to watch him."

"The Captain came below and looked at him. He felt his pulse and watched his breathing and went back to the bridge. I heard the bells of the annunciator ring and felt the engines pick up speed. They would have sent the message by now, typed out on a form, tapped out by Collins on his key,"

> "'RECOVERED P.J. FRANKLIN ALIVE.
> RETURNING TO PORT. ETA 1200.'"

"I stayed with P.J. Franklin all the way back to port, rubbing his hands and feet and I thought about the message. Just six words, some letters and a number that said all the people on the mainland wanted to know but didn't say anything about what had happened."

"There were just the two of us, me in the chair, him on the bench. I tried to feed him some coffee and put more blankets on him because his hands and feet were as cold as ice. Finally I heard the sea buoy go by, the change in pitch of the engines when we entered the harbor, and then the noises and yells from the deck."

"The Captain brought the ship in, you could tell that from just three bells taking her into the dock and then the long rings on the annunciator and the buzz of the phone in the engine room telling them, 'Finished with engines.'"

"Down in the wardroom I could hear them wind down, the sound lower and lower and stopped, and then the only sound from the generator and

that slowed, slowed some more, stopped, the lights dimmed and went out for a second and then went on again. The shore-tie was hooked up and we were fast to land, electric cable, water hose, mooring lines, telephone, attached with lines and hoses and cables that we wouldn't be pulling in or casting off."

"We weren't going anyplace that night, that day, of course it was day now, and I sat in the wardroom and waited for somebody to come for P.J. Franklin."

"They came, a wife and friends, an ambulance and medics, some reporters and they had trouble getting him onto the stretcher, up the ladder and out through the hatch. It isn't an easy thing to do."

"And then I went to look for Rowling. He was Officer of the Day and I told him to go home. I would stay aboard and take the watch and after everyone was gone, the Captain, John, the liberty section, I went back on the bridge."

"Up there it was all put away. The chart, dividers, pencils, the parallel rule were gone and tomorrow Rowling would start with his eraser and clean up the chart. Every line, square, and number until it was almost as good as new. The log was written up and the Rescue Report drafted and sitting on the yeoman's desk waiting to be typed."

"They would tell the story, the course changes, speeds, positions, wind speeds, barometric pressures and in a month there would be a new log with the old one stored away in a box and the Rescue Report filed away somewhere down in the basement of the Seventh Coast Guard District."

"I walked around up there and looked at the black screen of the radar, felt the cool spokes of the wheel and ran my hand over the gray bank of receivers and transmitters on the bulkhead. Then I leaned on the chart table and looked up at the wind speed indicator, the little black box the size of a clock. The hand was straight down. There was no wind."

"The storm had passed. Out on the

bridge-wing it was afternoon, cool and the sky was clear and I looked down to the fore-castle where the crew had saved themselves and a man, too, a hand for themselves and one for P.J. Franklin."

"The lines and raft, the emergency light, the stretcher were all back where they came from, in lockers or coiled and hung on a bulkhead. You won't believe it but I thought about the lifejacket, too, his lifejacket and wondered if I should go and try to find it. Look to see if the strap had almost parted, if the stitches were loose, but I didn't. What difference would it have made if they were, if the line had parted, if he had sunk in five hundred fathoms?"

"But there was nothing on the fore-castle except what was always there, the forty-millimeter cannon, stanchions, life-lines, the deck where the men had been and where the seas had come over the bow and broken, running white down the deck washing down the sides and out through the scuppers."

"The deck was clean. It was washed and scrubbed clean by the sea and cleaner than if you had gotten down on your hands and knees and done it yourself. I had never seen that deck so clean."

He went down on his haunches then and ran sand from his hand, letting it fall in a stream, scooping it up and letting it fall again. I sat cross-legged beside him and tried to think of something to say but there was nothing to say.

"You wonder if I would have done it?" he said. "If I'd gone forward to muster the crew and ask for a volunteer? ...But I knew no one would. No one would volunteer to go over the side into seas like that and in the dark, too. It was not something you volunteered for and you've heard what people say...."

"What?"

"Never volunteer, never volunteer for anything."

"I've heard plenty of people say it," I said and I had. I'd said it myself more than once.

"No one in his right mind would have done it and if no one volunteered, what would you do? Look up at the Captain on the bridge? Go back up there and tell him no one would go?"

"That was what I thought about in the wardroom when the Captain was telling us what we had to do. And then out there on deck with the ship rolling thirty, thirty-five, forty degrees with everyone holding on for their lives and you ask somebody to just let go and jump over the side?"

"Those people would wait for you to make up your mind, then for you to say it, yell it over the sound of the wind and the sea — 'All Right, I'll go.'"

"And after you'd said it hold up your

arms for the life-preserver like you were being fitted for a suit, walk over to the side if
you could get there, look at those troughs
where the sea pulled away when we rolled
with twenty or thirty foot peaks of water
coming at you, — and step over?"

"Would you do it?" he said.

"No," I said, "I wouldn't."

"You see? You would have to be a madman to do it, or someone who was forced.
The crew wasn't crazy, none of them, except maybe one, a seaman, but not the
Chief, definitely not the Chief and who
does that leave?"

"They must have laughed when John said,
"I'll go,' laughed and said to themselves,
'It's about time. Let him go. There's nine of
us like a firing squad and if no one volunteers he *has* to go. It comes with the little
gold bars."

"And there in port out on the bridge-
wing with the sun in the sky I felt my

storm was over, too. He didn't go because he wanted to. He didn't volunteer. He went because he had to. There was nothing courageous about that."

"There were ten people out there and one of them had to do it and when the other nine wouldn't, it was an order just as if the Captain had told him, or Congress, or the President of the United States. You don't get to be a hero by following an order you know is crazy, and with the sun full in my eyes I went below to my bunk and slept like a dead man."

IV

"And that's what you told her?" I said. "That's what she didn't understand. You wouldn't want a woman who couldn't understand that."

I was on my feet now and looking down at him. Finally I knew what he was talking about. I didn't know anything about knots and lines and storms at sea but I knew something about this.

It wasn't an excuse. She should have known he had done the right thing, what anyone in his right mind would have done. The ensign had gone all right but it was the same as if he had been pushed. He didn't have any choice, not where he came from. There it was a reflex, something they drummed into you, strike the knee in the right place and you jump, just point me and I'll march.

I said that to him, all of it, and he didn't answer. He only let the sand fall from his hand.

"You told her that?" I said.

"Yes."

"All of it? Just like you told it to me? That it couldn't have happened…not this side of King Arthur."

"Yes, I told her," he said, "…but not all…I told her all I knew…then."

"There was something else?"

"There was."

The last of the sand had fallen from his hand and he brushed the pile away, smoothed the place in front of him, and I said,

"It wasn't what you said?"

"No, it wasn't."

"Did John…?"

"Yes, he told me. At the very end he told me but I didn't understand it then."

"And now you do?"

"Yes, now I do, when it's too late, but you want to know what he said, don't you?"

His voice was different, aroused, as if he was excited, almost as if he looked forward to what he was going to say.

"You want to know what John told me, don't you," he said again.

"I do."

Wouldn't anyone, I thought, and because I was tired and light-headed from listening, I looked around to see if anyone was there.

"There were long, hot days under that sky after it was over. People talked about it but that got less and less and then not at all. They still looked at John, the crew did and the people who knew, and then that stopped too. We had routine calls, a dismasted yacht, a man out of gas off Cat Cay, nothing special. There was nothing any different from what we had always done."

"We got a letter of Commendation from the Commandant, the ship got one and John and the seaman who jumped into the raft. 'In the finest tradition…,' they said, all three said the same thing, only some of the words were different, 'You' for John and the seaman and 'Captain and crew' for the CGC TRAVIS."

"We went on Campeche Patrol, fourteen days out in the Gulf of Mexico waiting around for a shrimp boat to break down, water rations, salt water showers, food getting worse every day, and hotter than anything I've ever seen. You couldn't sleep. Not even naked on your bunk with the blowers going full-blast you couldn't sleep. It was fourteen days of hell and the sea as smooth as a griddle with us frying in the middle of it."

"I went out on the fantail and sat on a depth-charge rack to find some air, just sat

there in the dark with the only light coming from the port-holes in the mess deck.
They had a poker game going in there that
started with the patrol and wouldn't end
until we got back, people coming into the
game when their watch was over and getting up when their watch came by again."

"The lights were never off, three round
yellow eyes staring out over the stern you
could see for miles on that flat water. There
was no sea running. There isn't even any
tide down there, only a big, flat puddle of
hot water with the ship pushing along at
slow ahead going nowhere, doing nothing
except ending messages that said, 'Main-
taining Position' six times a day."

"I saw somebody else come out on the
fantail. He couldn't sleep either in the heat
and he sat down on the other rack. It was
John and I said, to be sociable,"

"'Hot.'"

"'It's hot all right.'"

"'Hot at night as it is in the day,'" I said and he nodded."

"Not much had been said since the rescue, only what we had to. I had my reasons and he must have had his. But he was never a talker. I never heard

him say five words to anybody except at the beginning when he came aboard and we talked those few times."

"We sat there for ten minutes and didn't say a word, he on one of the racks and me on the other. Finally I got up and went over, sat down and lit a cigarette."

"Want one?"

"No," he said and we sat and I smoked, just that one red speck in the dark and the three yellow ones shining out of the deck house. I finished my cigarette, flipped it overboard, and turned to him so I could see the side of his face. In the port-hole light it looked like there was only one side of his face and I said,"

"'Why did you do it?'"

"'What,' he said but he didn't move."

"''Why did you go in after him?'"

"'After who?' he said and I smiled at the 'who'. They didn't teach you everything at the Academy."

"'P.J. Franklin,' I said. 'Why did you go in after him?'"

"'Somebody had to.'"

"'Nobody said you had to.'"

"'It had to be somebody,' and when he said that he was looking into the dark and I was looking at him."

"'We could have put a man in the life-raft, two men, with a line on it. Drifted it down to him. The way we did with the others, with somebody in the raft.'"

"'If we could then that's the way the Captain would have done it,' and he looked at me for a moment the way he had on the bridge when I had said, 'If he has any chance at all.'"

"'Maybe he didn't think of it,' I said and he started to get up but I put my hand on him."

"'The Captain couldn't make anyone go, not in those seas.'"

"'No,' he said, 'he couldn't make anyone go.'"

"We sat on those racks on the flat sea and there wasn't even a wake behind us. I looked out over the stern and maybe I was getting heat stroke because though there were only some ripples on the water, it seemed to me as if there was something underneath. Something following along nearly underneath the ship but there was nothing I could see. And then I turned back to him and said,"

"'But you saved him,' and he nodded once, half a nod, enough to say 'yes' instead of nothing, and then he said,"

"'But the Captain found him.'"

"'Anyone could have found him.'"

"'No.'"

"'What do you mean, "no"?'"

"''Maybe anyone could have found him, but not anyone would have looked,'" and he got up from the depth-charge rack.

"'It's my watch,' he said, turned from me, and walked away."

"I followed him with my eyes. He blocked out the three yellow lights on the deck-house one after another until there was no one left on the fantail but me."

"The next day and the day after that he stayed away. If we had to be in the same place together, relieving a watch or sitting in the wardroom, he'd walk out as soon as I was there. And then, not even knowing it at first, I was following him."

"Up on the bridge, in the officer's quarters, even in the head. If the door to the stall was closed I waited. I stood there and washed my hands and waited for the door to open. Once when nobody came out I bent down, enough to see whose shoes were in there, and there was nobody."

"You can't hide on a ship, not forever, not for fourteen days on Campeche Patrol. We were too small a ship for that patrol anyway, canned food, fresh water rations, salt water showers, and the heat. It was a blue oven all day and a black one at night with nothing around us anywhere but the sea like a table and a shrimp boat or two off on the edge. Plenty of times you couldn't see anything around us at all, no boats, no clouds, nothing. You thought it was the end of the world and there was nobody else left anywhere."

"I'll tell you it was worse than storms, worse than thirty degree rolls and seventy knot winds, and it was beginning to make a difference. No one would talk. You gave orders in one syllable and got a grunt back and it was too much of an effort to do anything about it."

"But it didn't make any difference to me. I went around like something in a jungle, sweating, stalking him, waiting in passageways and outside hatches, waiting to get him alone where he couldn't get away. And finally I did, right back where I'd started."

'It was another night, hot and black and this time the blowers had broken down. They'd just given up, melted the windings in the heat, and down below it was a furnace."

"He was back on the fantail right where he'd been before but this time

I didn't sit down. I stood on the deck forward of him so he'd have to go around me to get away and this time there was no preamble either, nothing about the weather or smoking a cigarette. It was as if I had crept up behind and hit him with a rock and I said,"

"'You didn't have to go, nobody made you.'"

"I had to get him to say it, you see, to admit he was pushed over by that ring on his finger or those two little gold bars. And he looked up at me and then away, not at anything because there wasn't anything to see, not even the riding lights of the shrimp boats, and then he said it again,'"

"'Somebody had to.'"

"'You said that before.'"

"'Well, ...no one else would.'"

"'Couldn't you...?'" but I didn't finish because he said,"

"'That isn't true.'"

"'What isn't?' I said."

"'It isn't true that no one else would go.'"

"And now I didn't know if I wanted to hear any more of what he had to say or not. I hadn't thought he would say anything like that."

"'There was a seaman who would have gone,' he said, 'Moore, the gunner's mate striker. He would have gone.'"

"'And you didn't...did he volunteer?' It was all I could say, all I could think of to say and he took a breath, I think he took a breath, it was dark,"

"'I didn't let him.' he said."

"'You didn't let him?'"

"'No.'"

"'He volunteered...said he would go...?'"

"'Not in words. He didn't speak up. He didn't say he would go.'"

"'So how did you know he would?' I said. 'If he didn't say anything, if he didn't volunteer, how did you know he would?'"

"'Why do you want to know so badly?' he said and his voice had changed. He said it again,"

"'Tell me why you want to know.'"

"But I didn't know myself anymore or if I did I didn't want to say it, certainly not to him, not even to myself."

"'I just want to understand,' I said and he got up and walked to the rail, stood at the stern with his back to me as if what I'd said wasn't good enough. I had to raise the ante if I wanted to play and he was right, of course. It wasn't good enough."

"'It's not something you see every day, you know,' I said and was standing by his shoulder, the water below moving away from us."

"'It's only once in a lifetime,' I said, 'something you read about not something you see.'"

"He nodded, I think he nodded, and even there on the stern as far back on the ship as you can go, where nobody can see your face, he didn't want to tell me. He was already lying, lying about the seaman who would have gone. He couldn't admit he had done it because he was backed into a corner."

"Up there on the fore-castle with nine men around him, six more watching from the bridge, twenty-five down below waiting to hear what happened, with a ring on his finger and gold bars on his shoulders he was in a corner like a rat."

"He was in one now, on the stern of the ship with only one man behind him and the sea around both of us. He was caught, don't you see, and couldn't run. He had lied once already and once was more than enough for me."

"'Why do you keep asking me?' he said."

"But it didn't make any difference what he said now. I might even have smiled a little in the dark because when he was finished with whatever he was going to tell me, whatever he had made up his mind to say, I was going to tell <u>him</u> why he had done it."

"'All right,' he said and with both hands out in front of him he leaned his weight on the rail."

"'I'll tell you how I knew Moore would go, what it was like up there on the fore-castle, but after I do will you leave me alone? Will you stop asking questions?'"

"He meant it. I could hear he meant it. Whatever he was going to say was his story, how he would always tell it."

"'Yes,' I said. 'You tell me what happened up there and I'll never say another word.'"

"He told you then," I said.

"Yes, he told me."

"What you said to her?"

"Yes, what I said to her, all of it, just the way he told me."

"And what he told you wasn't true."

"No, it wasn't," he said. "It wasn't what I thought he would say and it wasn't the truth. It wasn't either of them."

He stood up. He stood up and I sat down. I had been standing and didn't know it and I was tired, my feet, my legs, all of me was tired and still I didn't know, and even more, I didn't know what I could say even when I knew."

"I told her about him, what he had done

and why, but my God what happened between us wasn't because I wouldn't go over
the side after P.J. Franklin. Do you see it
wasn't?"

"It was because...it was because of the
reason I told her. My God I was proud of
telling her, proud I had put the card I
thought the most of on the table and
turned it over. Because, you see, what I told
her about me was the truth."

It was not a word I wanted to hear. I had
known it was coming but I didn't want to
hear it. For a long time it was a word I
never wanted to hear again.

"Why in the name of God did you tell
her at all?" I said. "You didn't have to, no
one made you," and because it was something I should never have said, I said
something worse,"

"She didn't make you," and at that moment I thought of the hare already
running, already doomed, and the dogs still

playing in the courtyard.

"I told her because of what John had said."

"Who...the ensign...not him surely?"

"Yes, him."

"Back on the fantail he was looking right at me, arms out, hands on the railing, and he said,"

"'You don't understand.'"

"Almost anything would have been better because I did understand, more than understand, I knew, and I almost laughed right in his face. I wanted to whisper it, tell him in his ear, but I didn't. I held it in as if I was holding my breath underwater because he had to say it you see. He had to lie so I could tell him the truth."

It was back again, the word. There was another word, what truth was, and I was sure that it was coming, too.

"'What I did wasn't anything,' John said, 'not really.'"

"'That's not what everybody thinks,' I said, 'not what everybody will always think.'"

"'I know,' he said."

"'You'll probably get a medal. You saw the Commandant's letter, "...by your meritorious service...in the finest tradition." They give medals for those things.'"

"'I saw it.'"

"'It'll follow you around for the rest of your life,' I said. 'Those things do, you know. People know and they tell others. People will always know.'"

"He nodded with his head down and I wanted to grab him. I wanted to take him by that corn-colored hair and hold his head up so he had to look at me."

"'Well?' I said. 'What's wrong with a medal? Wouldn't you like to have one?' and he raised his head,"

"'I did it because it had to be done. Somebody had to do it and I did.'"

"'But you said there was somebody else – Moore – you said he would have gone but you wouldn't let him.'"

"'Yes, Moore would have gone. He wants to go to the Academy.'"

"'Well, why didn't you let him go if you knew he would? The Captain said to ask for volunteers. Did you ask? Did you say, "Are there any volunteers?"'"

"I had my hand on John by now. I was holding him."

"'No,' he said. 'I didn't say that, not exactly that. I said who wants to go or something like it.'"

"'And nobody spoke up?'"

"'Nobody did but you couldn't have heard anyone if they did. They probably didn't even hear me. It was blowing a gale, you know. You could hardly talk on the bridge, remember, and out there on the fore-castle you couldn't talk at all.'"

"'I just yelled something – 'Who wants to

go?' And nobody said anything but I was looking at Moore when I said it. He knew what it was and I could tell by the way he looked at me that he would go. All I would have to do was point.'"

"'And you didn't?'"

"I was stunned by what he said because it didn't sound like a lie and if it was a lie, why would he tell it? It sounded like the truth, not the one I was ready to tell him but a different one, another truth altogether."

"'I was frightened to death,' he said, 'out of my wits but I didn't let Moore go. I turned away and let the Chief put the life-jacket on me.'"

"I tell you what he told me was as crazy as everything else. The rain coming at us across the water like it was shot out of a cannon, those squares on the chart that never got to be squares, that just kept getting bigger, and the ship rolling more every time we changed course ready to roll us over."

"He was mad and I was too standing out there in the middle of the Gulf of Mexico listening to him, but the most insane thing, the strangest of all was that I believed him. He had done it himself. It had nothing to do with having to."

"All by himself for some reason, some craziness, he wanted to go into that ocean and try to save an old man and probably be lost himself, and for what? …So Moore wouldn't have to do it? …I couldn't fathom it and when I thought that I laughed, I really did…couldn't fathom it?"

"But now I had both hands on him and I said,"

"'My God — Why?' and then he told me. He told me something that would change everything."

I was afraid of it. Though I knew something like it was coming, still I was afraid.

"'Because I wanted to...I wanted to do something,' he said, 'I don't know how to say it...something as good as the Captain had done,' and I said what anyone would have said,"

"'You mean "as well",' but he came back at me,"

"'I know the difference.'"

"'Between "well" and "good"?' but I knew it was the wrong thing to say."

"'Yes. I know the difference as well as you do,' and I dropped my hands from where I had been holding him."

"'I meant what I said,' and his voice was like ice."

"'I mean something "as good" as the Captain finding him. Everyone wanted to quit. All you wanted to do was go home because you were sure the man was gone and we would never find him. You were sure, weren't you?'"

Well, I thought to myself, finally it was

here or 'they' were here: 'truth' and 'good' were here and weren't they always? I was going to tell him what I thought of them, along with 'beauty' but he was nodding his head and said,

"I told him yes, what else could I do? I had to because it was what I had thought all that time we searched, because no one could have found him except for luck."

"'It was luck,' I said, 'just luck that we found him.'"

"'*We* didn't find him. There was no "we" about it. The Captain found P.J. Franklin,' and I remembered I had said the same thing. And there was no 'we' about saving him, either. He was right, the Captain had found him, and Stone, standing at the wheel with his two feet in the same place for fifteen hours. The two of them had found him, a head and a pair of hands."

"'And you saved him,' I said, 'to do something…"as good"…as the Captain?'"

"'Yes,' and he looked at me as if I was there for the first time."

"'Now,' he said, 'can I ask you a question?' and I wanted to turn and run. I wanted to run up into the bow or down into the engine room. I wanted to run anywhere."

They were here with a vengeance, truth and goodness were, and I thought to myself, far better to have the hunting dogs pursuing you.

"'Why didn't you go?' he said. 'You had the chance. The Captain asked you first.'"

"It was my turn to look away into the dark and say again because there was nothing else to say,"

"'I was sure no one would volunteer, no one would go over after him,' and I waited for him to say it. I even wondered how he would."

"'And you were afraid it would have to be you.'"

"That was the way he said it, the way I would have if it had been me."

"'Yes,' I said, 'that's why.'"

"I left him on the fantail after that and went down to my bunk and lay there in the heat. The blowers came back on again later and I never heard them. I was late for my watch and Rowling had to call me."

"The next day and the day after that John was a different person. He called for chipping hammers and wire brushes and paint, new lines for the davits, man overboard, collision and fire drills. And there weren't any grunts from the crew, either. It was, 'Yes, sir, Mr. Gregory.'"

"They didn't like it but he had done something they would never do and with that after your name things get done. He had gone into an ocean and saved a man and now he looked it. Nobody would, nobody could, forget it now."

"To do something, 'as good as the Captain,' and it was just what you said, 'not this side of King Arthur.' I believed him about the seaman, Moore, too, because I watched them. I watched the both of them and it had to be true, nearly too good to be true and I almost laughed at that. He had done it and now I knew why and that, of course, was why I had to tell her."

A chill went through me then. It was wind from the southeast with the beginning of day. It blew along the beach with dried weed scuttling along the sand and out in front of us the seas were starting.

"I had to tell her the truth, too, don't you see? It was a chance, a second one, one I thought I would never have. Not to be a hero, not that, but to do something...."

I was cold, shivering, both the wind and I were cold and in the east the sky was light.

"To do something right – to tell the truth – but would you know what that means?"

"I know," I said with my arms wrapped

around my knees. Now the dogs had left the castle yard and were barking in the woods.

"I know," I said again.

"All right," he said. "I told her – 'to be good' – Do you understand that? I thought because it meant so much to me, it would mean so much more to her."

"For once in my life I would have done the right thing and done it for her, you see? I said I was frightened, didn't go down on that fore-castle even with the bars on my shoulders that said I should. Then I didn't have behind me what the Captain had, but I did with her. You see that, don't you — to do for her what I thought was good?"

"And you lost her," I said in a whisper so cold now I couldn't feel my fingers.

"Yes," he said. "I lost her trying to do what they had done. It was a conspiracy of goodness."

V

And that, of course, should have been the end of it and it might have been. I could have left it that way and said nothing, forgotten what he hadn't told me and let it hide in what he had. The error of a friend you don't mention at the time and then forget because it's someone else's turn to talk. But I didn't forget and because I thought if he told me about the girl he would tell me about that, too, I said,

"Tell me about her."

And he did but it was something, except at the end, I could have told him myself.

She was different from everyone, he said, especially her eyes. There was some gold in the brown and she was small and looked frail but she wasn't.

Once he had said that to her, that she was

frail, and she said he should try to blow her over and he tried and couldn't. She just stood there with her hands on her hips and her brown hair tied in a ribbon.

And there was a time somewhere when they stood on a cliff with the seagulls below and the sea below them and she said to him, "Do you think someday the day will come when the day won't come?"

He said she spoke like that, the way she had said that the island was antique in a way, that it had seen better days and liked them better, too. Once there was the beginning of an argument and she had said it was a misunderstanding, that they should stop, because words were not strong enough to survive misunderstanding.

It was here on the island he had told her. He had told her what he thought was the truth, about himself and it was, but not the truth about everything.

They had been happy here walking on the

beaches and staying at the hotel. She even knew the bartender's name and she was always the first one to wake up in the morning to see it all begin she said. They held hands everywhere they went so that on Sunday when they went to church some people smiled and had to walk around them on the way.

The church was wood and old and white and there was a piano but no one played. The preacher was black with white hair and stood behind a table at the front with only a Bible on it. And standing there next to me on that beach he took the deepest of breaths and said it was all like the picture of an old-fashioned wedding.

It was then I thought that for a long time in our lives love is what we have instead of God, and then, of course, we have nothing.

He thought it was right. She deserved to know the truth and would think more of him because he told her. She didn't understand, he said, but perhaps she did. She could have understood more than he knew, much more. I asked him if they had talked about it later, after he had told her, and they had. They had talked about it once but not again.

"'And would you do it now?' she said. 'Would you go into the ocean after some-one...now?'"

"'I would,' he said. 'I would in a minute without thinking twice.'"

It was there that he was wrong. He didn't know how much more he had meant than he had said.

But they were together and he was happy, happier than he had ever been and he talked of having plans, getting married, looking for a place to live and one day she was gone.

There was a note from her, part of a poem, and some seashells on the table.

"When the storms break for him
May the trees shake for him
Their blossoms down;
And in the night that he is troubled
May a friend wake for him
So that his time be doubled;
And at the end of all loving and love
May the Man above
Give him a crown."

He spoke the words and a look came over his face I could see in the early light. It was the look of someone who doesn't know what has happened to them and he said,

"Do you know that poem?"

"No. I've never heard it before."

"I wish I knew the rest of it," he said. "It was the kind of thing she knew, poems, and she knew them from beginning to end. But she didn't know the end of what I told her. She only knew why I hadn't done it. She never knew why he had."

"She didn't have to know me the way I had always been. She could know me now the way I am because I'm not the same person anymore. What the Captain did and what John finally told me changed things, they changed me, don't you see?"

I saw and she had seen, too. He had his banner, his bridge to guard, his message to deliver, even his rescue, all things that come before all other things. He was right about her. She was different. With those eyes she was different enough to see a future he didn't see, a voyage together better not taken. The rest came like a dropped spool, rolled, unwound and stopped underneath in an unreachable dark.

"My time aboard ship was nearly over. The Captain asked me about John, about how much he had changed, and I didn't know what to say. I said something about growing up and gaining his confidence and he said John had the makings of a fine officer and would have his own command one day."

"And finally it was my last day. My bags were packed. The steward's mate had taken them ashore and I had my orders in my hand. I gave them to the watch at the gangway and he wrote them in the log:

> 1400 – Lieutenant Francis O. Farrington, Service Number
> 40884, USCGR, departed under order number 867/3001
> to Commander, Seventh Coast Guard District for discharge from active duty.

He handed them back to me and that was all it took for me to leave the Coast Guard Cutter Travis forever."

"I stepped up onto the gangplank and wondered how it was going to feel to salute the flag for the last time — and John was there. He was standing by the rail, Officer of the Day, with his clean cap cover on. I was going to have to salute him, too, one for the Officer of the Day and one for the flag."

"I raised my hand to my cap and he did too, and smiled. With two more steps to go before I left the ship and stood on land I stopped and saluted again, this one for the flag. A snappy one in the finest tradition and as I brought my hand down I waved. I waved to the ship, to John, to everything that had happened and with my thumb stuck out it could have been a blessing."

"And John said something. It was only loud enough for me to hear,

'Don't worry,' he said, 'they'll never find you either,' and he walked away toward the fore-castle along a deck so clean you could dance a jig on it."

It was easy to imagine a day in brilliant sun when he stood and saluted, everything bright in white and tan and brass. Someone could have painted a picture, it was the kind of thing you could paint a picture of, "*AVE ATQUE VALE*" or something like that. But the people passing by to look at it hanging on a wall would never know what kind of farewell they were seeing there.

"For a long time after I walked down that gang-way I thought about what John had said and never understood it. I didn't know what he meant when he said it or for a long time afterwards. It's hard to believe but whenever I saw a ship or a flag I would remember it, because it didn't ring, do you see? It had a hollow sound a long time after like a cracked bell."

We walked down to the water then for the last time, stood a yard away from it, and I stood beside him. I didn't know what John had meant either. There must have been more than he had said and there was. There was not much more but there was enough.

"After I told her, brought her here and told her, after it was done and she was gone I tried to forget about it all. I couldn't, of course, not with coming here every year I couldn't. I came because, — well, you know, stranger things have happened but she was never here and I never had the chance to tell her what he meant."

He turned to me and put both his hands on my shoulders as if even now, after our long night together, I too would run away.

"What he had meant," he said. "I thought about it sitting in that room in the hotel and walking this beach. I even went back to the old church with the piano nobody played and sat in the same chairs."

"He'd said, 'Don't worry, they'll never find you either,' and finally I understood. Standing right here on this beach I knew, as if someone had come up behind me and taken a blindfold off my eyes."

"When I walked down the gang-way and

he said that, it was <u>his</u> blessing, a message for me in a world that measured you for life, that ran a tape around your crotch and asked what size hat you wanted to wear. He'd gone over the side after P.J. Franklin so he would never have to do anything like it again."

"Not for duty or Moore or, my God, to do something 'as good as the Captain' but so he would never be asked again in his life because who would ask him? Who would because somehow he would have already told them, or somebody would, that he had already done it for P.J. Franklin. And done it for duty, goodness, country, the ship, for the Captain and not because he knew what he was, just like you or me. He did it because rather than be found he wanted never to be looked for."

He was finished. There was nothing more to tell.

We walked back to the hotel and it was

there I left him, but before I started down
the King's Highway in the light of another
day I stopped us. I wanted to say something, some last thing for him and certainly
not how she had understood far better than
he knew, but all I could do was offer my
hand.

He took it, we shook hands for the third
time, for luck I suppose. With the sun up
the sky opened like a scallop shell and over
his shoulder to the west of the island I could
see the seas come on, lines of them, legions.

*   *   *

I went back to Bimini twice to see if he
was there, but he wasn't. I waited a week
the second time and walked around the island, along the beach where he and I had
walked. I stood and looked out over the sea
and knew I shouldn't have come. No banner had waved or trumpet sounded because

it wasn't me he had told at all. It had been her, something perhaps he didn't need to tell her now and that was all I gave him, only that of all there was to give. I had a drink in the bar, sat at the table, and they hadn't heard from him either, but of course he could have been there at another time.